Drake's Bay

by ANTHONY R. MILLS

FITHIAN PRESS, SANTA BARBARA

1996

Published by Fithian Press
A division of Daniel and Daniel, Publishers, Inc.
Post Office Box 1525
Santa Barbara, CA 93102

Lyrics from the songs "Big Iron" and "Powder Blue Sky"
by Bob Moore used with permission.

Book design by Eric Larson

LIBRARY OF CONGRESS CATALOGING-IN-PUBLICATION DATA
    Mills, Anthony R., date
    Drake's bay / Anthony R. Mills.
        p.   cm.
    ISBN 1-56474-158-3
    I. Title.
PS3563.I42292D7   1996
813'.54—dc20   95-37390
                                         CIP

For all who have known the Sea Swallow.

Introduction

When Sir Francis Drake and the crew of the *Golden Hind* sailed north along what is now known as the west coast of the United States and Canada during the spring of 1579, he was in search of a passage to the Atlantic Ocean. It is estimated that he went as far north as Vancouver, British Columbia, before adverse weather forced him to turn back southward. On June 17, 1579, he reached a "faire and good Baye." Exactly where this bay was has been the subject of much speculation in the intervening centuries.

If the *Golden Hind*'s log books could be located, the dispute over the location of Drake's "faire and good Baye" could be resolved. But when Drake returned to England on September 26, 1580, he gave the logs and charts of his voyage to Queen Elizabeth I, and they have not been seen since. A possible explanation for this is that some of the charts were confiscated from Spanish galleons, and that Elizabeth was playing an artful game with Spain to assure the Spanish ambassador that Drake had been an independent operator, a pirate, rather than a privateer. When Elizabeth paid a visit to the *Golden Hind* after a nine-month delay, she commanded Drake to kneel, but she would not knight him, for to do so might have sparked a war that was to take place during the summer of 1588. Therefore the English virgin queen gave the sword to a French envoy, who knighted Drake on her behalf.

Charts and accounts of the voyage that have been made since then have been based upon second-hand information. In 1589 Judocus Hondius made a world map that traced Drake's voyage, and his map identified a "Portus Nove Albionis" that closely resembled what is today known as Drake's Bay.

In 1936, however, a man strolling along San Francisco Bay near San Quentin found a brass plate roughly the size of this book, which, when cleaned, was seen to contain an inscription in Elizabethan English. Soon after this discovery another man came forward and claimed that he had originally found the plate near Drake's Bay and tossed it into the trunk of his automobile and forgotten about it. Two years later, while repairing a flat tire, he came upon the plate and, not thinking much of it, threw it away near the spot where it was discovered in 1936.

The plate's authenticity is still debated despite extensive scientific research. Today this unique artifact is on display in the Bancroft Library at the University of California at Berkeley.

The text of the plate reads as follows:

BEE IT KNOWNE VNTO ALL MEN BY THESE PRESENTS

IVNE 17 1579

BY THE GRACE OF GOD AND IN THE NAME OF HERR

MAIESTY QVEEN ELIZABETH OF ENGLAND AND HERR

SVCCESSORS FOREVER I TAKE POSSESSION OF THIS

KINGDOME WHOSE KING AND PEOPLE FREELY RESIGNE

THEIR RIGHT AND TITLE IN THE WHOLE LAND VNTO HERR

MAISTIES KEEPING NOW NAMED BY ME AN TO BEE

KNOWN VNTO ALL MEN AS NOVA ALBION.

FRANCIS DRAKE

PART ONE

The Sea Swallow

"HAVE YOU EVER NOTICED A FLICKERING light on the beach at night?" asked a Coast Guard sentry of the other attendant on night watch at the Coast Guard station located on the western end of Drake's Bay, about forty miles north of San Francisco.

"Some kids, probably, on their motorcycles," was the response.

"It's only one light, though. That's odd. Sometimes I see this light by the state park, then by the cliffs. It's too slow to be a motor bike."

Getting up from behind the desk, he asked, "Where do you see this light, anyway?"

"Over there by the cliffs, on the north end of the bay."

"Let me see those binoculars." Reviewing the slopes at the northern end of the bay, he said, "Could be anything." Finally he located the glimmer of the light in question, which appeared to be fading behind a ravine. "They're not supposed to be camping out over there. A family probably—lost a wallet or a pet dog or cat. Has anyone called?"

"No calls. Didn't Randolph claim to have seen a strange light," he thought a moment, "and didn't he say he saw an old man wearing a big top hat by the beach in the fog?"

Returning to his desk, the other answered, "Yeah. I remember something like that. Didn't they accuse him of hallucinating up here?"

"Transferred him to a buoy tender in the Aleutians, I believe."

"Want to call the park service?"

"Somebody could be lost out there, you know."

He dialed the number. "Yes. We are from the Point Reyes Coast Guard Station at Drake's Bay, and we have been tracking an unknown light."

He glanced out the window facing a northerly direction to locate the light's latest position. "It's by the beach now. We have surmised that someone could be lost or in some sort of difficulty out there. Do you have any information on this?" There was a pause. "What you are telling us is that on a clear moonless night this is a frequent report?" He hung up the telephone receiver. "He told me if we find out anything to keep them posted."

Breezy's Resort

Moored to a weathered dock constructed of driftwood at Breezy's Marina just south of Napa on the Napa River, a schooner built on a thirty-six-foot lifeboat hull was prepared for a two-week commercial fishing excursion. Its twin fifty-five-gallon diesel tanks, which propelled the schooner's proven Navy model four-cylinder gray Marine Budda engine, had been filled to the brim. Quantities of ice in a large Styrofoam chest contained frozen anchovy bait in sealed plastic bags, and was stowed in the boat's forward hold. Ten-, twenty- and forty-pound shots of lead balls to weigh down trolling cables the desired depth were also situated in the forward hold, along with various sized army-green shovels, fishing angles, and an array of tackle, lures of all shapes, designs and colors. Nylon drop lines rolled around a hollow cardboard tube still wrapped in its saran cover and hooks were disorderly scattered about. In the wheel house lures with chrome flashers, some with colored feathers, green, red and white, were stuck by their barbed hooks in the Styrofoam insulation where it was exposed by the portholes and windows.

Fresh water stored in plastic water jugs, dry stores, eggs, some milk, cheese, fruit and vegetables were stored aboard; there were also a few packets of lunch meat and a few narrow sticks of salami especially for Johannesen, the Norwegian artist, who favored this type of meat. The crew of the *Sea Swallow* wanted to ensure that this expedition would be successful.

While waiting in line at the supermarket that afternoon, Tod, a nephew of the Colonel, captain of the *Sea Swallow*, had picked up an adventure magazine and thrown it into the cart with the other items being purchased. The magazine, like everything else acquired for the trip, made it to the *Sea Swallow*, but was not placed where it could be readily located.

Cylinder-shaped single dry-cell batteries were purchased for one flashlight. But kerosene for two lanterns and a portable stove would have to be purchased at a hardware store. If not, the schooner's fuel would have to do.

In the barroom at Breezy's Marina sixty or so feet from the docks, a "Bon Voyage" party for the commercial fishing venture was in progress, contrary to the halcyon *Sea Swallow*, which was gently nudging her makeshift dock. The river rats and driftwood derelicts as well as part-time nonconformists were here in force; the free food on a side table by the window facing east was a strong draw to them.

In the midst of the eating, drinking, smoking and talking, a few patrons had fallen asleep on the north end of the building by a wood stove; Rolf, the Russian standing in the middle of the building a few feet behind the stools by the bar counter, was spouting out a monologue, gaining momentum whenever he noticed that he was the scant object of somebody's attention.

"Let me tell you that I have seen this many—yes—many times before! Have you ever heard of the *IF*? Johannesen and his goofy cohort Fusco wanted to sail to Easter Island. I provided for them with all of the necessary provisions: the food, the water, the plywood." His voice was rising noticeably in volume. "Clothes, the canvas, even the boat! It was I who supplied them the *IF*. Even got them a bottle of cognac and pith helmets. How far did they get?"

"What's he flapping his jaws about now?" asked someone at the bar counter.

"Who knows? Speak up, Rolf. We can't hear you."

"Do you know how far they got?" He spoke to the crowd as if they were listening or cared. "Not two miles past the rock pile. On the mud they were found with 500 pounds of macaroni stuffed aboard. But who here tonight remembers my generosity? The Colonel should know better. With this crew he is doomed to failure. Mark my word. Just like the *IF,* my friends. Just like the *IF.* Doomed to failure."

"If *IF* were a skiff," exclaimed someone at the bar, "we'd get a fifth, we'd go for a boat ride and then we'd…"

"Hard liquor is not allowed in here," informed the bartender.

"No. The *IF* wasn't a skiff," corrected Rolf. "It was an old-time twenty-six-foot whale boat. One of those wooden things you pick up at those military auctions." He indicated with his head and left hand southward toward Mare Island Naval Shipyard.

The skipper of the *Sea Swallow,* the Colonel, entered the barroom, and Rolf asked him, "Colonel, would you have any use for a bottle of cognac?" Before the Colonel could give a reply, Rolf continued with his verbal discourse. "You are doomed to failure. History shall repeat itself."

"Get him a beer," offered someone sitting at the bar counter so that it would serve as a pacifier.

At this point Johannesen, the First Mate of the *Sea Swallow,* seated at the bar counter, and Rolf caught sight of each other, and the spouting Russian snidely asked the Colonel, "How many pounds of macaroni are you going to take along this time?"

"You've got a beer coming, Rolf," interjected the bartender.

"Whom must I thank for this magnanimous gesture?"

"It's on the house," answered the bartender.

Raising the glass mug full of beer, Rolf offered a toast, "To the house," then proceeded to consume the alcoholic beverage.

A bleached blond with darting black eyes, native of England, who by her own admission engaged in a form of sorcery euphemistically labeled "white magic," was listening to Rolf's declarations and was becoming rather inspired.

Bob Moore, a tall, genuinely personable Army veteran, retired electrician, and local recording artist, took a bar stool next to where the Colonel and Rolf were standing and began tuning his guitar. The stringed musical instrument, tuned in accordance to the musician's excellent perceptive sense of pitch, began a rendition of a folk tune he had composed himself:

> *Down a lonely railroad track,*
> *Where my memory takes me back,*
> *To where the smoke poured from the stack*
> *Of the big iron on the track.*
>
> *Oh she's mighty long and high;*
> *As the steam goes flashing by,*
> *She's a big iron on the track,*
> *With smoke pouring from the stack.*

Moore's voice began to soar as it stretched across the refrain of the song.

> *Big iron. Big iron.*
> *She's a big rim on the track,*
> *She moves like a lightning flash,*
> *Her dry wheels seem to fly,*
> *As the big irons storm on by.*
> *You can hear the engines groan…"*

Johannesen walked up to Moore and simply stated, "We're ready."

Moore laid the guitar alongside the wall by the window and followed Johannesen.

Most of the patrons at the bar counter were entering an adjacent room to the ballroom at the southern end of the building where a billiard table was located at the center of the room and where two heavy banged-up old-time upright pianos were also located, one on the south end of the building and the other on the western side of the building. Sitting on the billiard table facing the east in a folded-leg, oriental meditating position with a white veil placed over her head, holding in her left hand a thin crimson-lit incense stick that was emitting a burning fragrant odor, sat the sorceress. She was surrounded by thirteen lit incensed candles; the flames at the end of the wicks did not flicker in the draftless room. Her incense smoke had merged with the fumes of the onlooker's cigarette smoke, adding to her beguiling disguise. After sufficient quiet had been sustained with the assistance of some members of the audience, "Hush! She needs it to be quiet," the Sorceress began to speak in low, foreboding tones.

"Where is everybody?" asked Betty, proprietress of the waterfront establishment, who had entered the business side of the building.

"In the other room," answered the bartender, pointing with his right hand, a cigarette wedged between his fingers.

"What's going on?" She walked to the room's entrance. Before entering the room, Betty could see the witch holding the customers spellbound, which in itself was not what angered her. She adamantly prohibited any necromancy/chicanery practice of any kind on her property; among other things it gave her bad vibrations, as they say.

"I told them not to bring her here again," said Betty to herself. "What does it take for them to get the message?" She addressed the bartender, "Who did she come with? Johannesen?"

"I guess," shrugged the bartender.

"Where's the broom? I'm going to give her something she won't forget," she said as she re-entered the back room.

After humming herself into a trance, the witch began to foretell the upcoming adventure:

Many frustrations there will be,
For this crew while they're at sea.

The cantoress of the seance was surprising herself with the silly rhyme and meter in which her forebodings were flowing.

Big waves and hard luck will be your lot.

"What else is new?" thought Moore.

Then with renewed vigor the witch pointed to Johannesen and proclaimed, with a voice that startled Betty, who was keeping a close watch over the seance with a broom in her hands from a shadow in the doorway, "You with the rotten teeth—no belief!"

That did it as far as Johannesen was concerned. He began to condemn her in his native Norwegian. *"Heks! Spinne av falsh foretelling! Løgn. Falsh prophet!"*

Duty-bound to defend the woman's honor, Moore entered the immediate situation. "I will not tolerate any man using that tone of voice in the presence of a lady. I demand that you apologize!"

In came Betty, swinging the broom at Johannesen and Moore. "I told you not to bring her here," the bar owner emphasized her statement with a swat of the broom. "I don't allow this type of thing."

Another swat of the broom went to the two crew members of the *Sea Swallow.*

"We didn't do nothing!" exclaimed Johannesen.

"You sound like a broken record, Johannesen," she said with still another swat of the broom.

Rolf was informing himself, "It is time to vacate the premises forthwith, to a safer location," walking in the direction of the bar counter.

The sorceress, with her eyes closed, returned to her humming to conjure spirits and was impervious as to what was happening in front of her.

"And as for you," declared Betty to the sorceress and pointing at her, "the next time I find you here," then pointing and talking to Johannesen, "you're both going for a saltwater swim. Now, I'm telling you for the last time, Johannesen—the last time—to keep your weird friends away from here." She walked away, then turned around and started anew, "And that Fusco! He wrote me out over seventy-five dollars of bad checks!"

Johannesen was trying to offer an explanation, "I—I can't help how these people act. What can I do?"

The sorceress then focused her mind on reality, got to her feet and jumped from the billiard table to the floor and began to scream in piercing soprano tones, running around the billiard table screeching, "They're going to drown me! They're going to drown me! Listen to them! Help! Isn't anyone going to do anything? I can't swim." More screams filled the air as the onlookers covered their ears. "They're going to drown me!"

The bartender put two quarters into the jukebox and struck the numbers 1-4-9, and Bob Moore's phonograph recording of "Big Iron" began to play. A series of train whistles, a harmonica that joins the musical poem's preparatory movement, caught Moore's ear.

"That's my song." He went into the barroom, picked up his guitar, which was leaning along the wall near the window pane facing the east, sat on the bar stool that was a few feet away from where the other stools were from the bar counter, and began to accompany and sing along with his recording:

Down a lonely railroad track
Where my memory takes me back
To where the smoke poured from the stack
Of the big iron on the track....

"Johannesen! This is my last warning! Who else but me," she threw her hands in the air, "would put up with this?"

"Oh-oh, folks. Here we go again. The last warning has been issued," said the heavy-set customer wearing his customary overcoat who was standing in the doorway in between the two rooms.

Moore stopped playing his guitar and singing, and yelled out to the next room where the excitement was in progress and where, holding a refilled glass mug of beer, Rolf was once again a spectator. "Don't let her on the boat," meaning the *Sea Swallow*. "Remember the last time we had a witch aboard?"

The following sentences from the Colonel confirmed Betty's dubious vibrations. "We ran aground. Couldn't get off the mud for six hours. Crew got into a fight."

"Sounds like pure malarkey. Figment of the imagination—or this," commented Rolf, raising his three-fourths-filled beer mug.

The Colonel, not wanting to be a part of the continuing nonsense that was taking place, situated himself on the perimeter of the action in the south room by the upright piano by the south wall and at the edge of the piling-supported wooden building.

The Colonel was fast asleep in his army sleeping bag in the wheelhouse when Rolf, Johannesen and Tod finally stumbled aboard like a herd of buffalo.

To guarantee himself a place to stretch out his legs, Moore was making ready his sleeping bag in his station wagon. Soon enough he would have to share the amenities of shipboard life that would detectably affect his amiable character.

At 5:30 ante meridian the Colonel pulled himself out of his sleeping bag, spread it out, closed the zipper and began to fold the sleeping bag into itself, tucking the zipper inside. He rolled the sleeping bag up beginning at the head until it was a neat portable size, secured the rolled military-green sack of cotton that holds duck and goose down with bow knots by two pairs of straps at the foot end of the sleeping bag, and stored it in a corner in the wheelhouse.

The two other crew members, Johannesen and Tod, were still incapacitated in varying degrees of sleep, as was the loquacious passenger, Rolf; Moore was also safely dreaming away in his station wagon.

The Colonel went straight to work. On the aft deck of the *Sea*

Swallow he lifted up a four-foot-square wooden hatch that led to the engine room—or, more accurately described, the engine compartment. He then connected the positive battery cable to the positive battery posts, permitting the current needed to turn over the Budda diesel engine to flow. The positive battery cable was disconnected as a safety device against the battery current draining, and against any would-be fool who would take the schooner for a joy ride—or a more serious threat, a thief.

The wires that closed the circuit between the battery and the starter motor were connected, which turned the starter motor; this rotated the pendix gear clockwise, forcing the pendix gear out to mesh with the ring gear on the flywheel, which turned over the diesel engine. When the diesel engine turned over, the fuel pump injected diesel fuel into the cylinders. High compression and heat in the cylinder combined with the spray of diesel fuel caused a controlled explosion, which forced one piston down and its counter piston up, ad infinitum.

Letting the engine idle for ten minutes, the Colonel returned to the wheelhouse, where Rolf, the first to crawl out of the cabin looking grotesque, gave testimony to the previous night's activities.

"Where are we going, Colonel?"

"Well, good morning, Rolf," answered the Colonel cheerfully. "How do you feel?"

"As to be expected," as his cranium, neck and upper body moved in acknowledgment of the question. "And yourself?"

"Me? How do I feel? Just fine. You fellows had quite a time last night."

"Yeah. Quite a time last night."

"What happened to the witch?"

"She called a taxi. Ah, Colonel, where are we going?"

"Bodega Bay. We'll see how the fishing…"

Rolf in the meantime was moving his right index finger of his right hand in the negative direction.

"…is up there. If not, we might head out to Eureka or even

Crescent City. I come from up that way, you know. On the way down we could stop off at Drake's Bay. Want to come?"

"No, no, Colonel." Glancing behind himself to the two sleeping occupants in the cabin, and a dog, and then toward Moore's station wagon, he shook his head. "This type of thing isn't for me. With this crew? And a dog? No! No! I'm going to have to pass this one up."

"A dog?" thought the Colonel. "What's he talking about? There isn't a dog aboard." Then the colonel said out loud, "We could drop you off at the Boat Center."

"I'll go along with that. Need some help casting off?"

The athletic retired Colonel jumped on the dock and got the spring line, then the bow line, then the stern line off, and he cast them onto the deck of the schooner. He then went to the stern of the schooner and pushed out as far as he could without falling into the water. He then sprang aboard, pushed a stiff lever forward which engaged the transmission ahead, which turned the short shaft and large work screw in a clockwise motion, and gave the throttle three-fourths power, since the bow of the *Sea Swallow* was facing north—upstream. The Colonel gave the wheel a hard right rudder, and within five minutes the schooner with its skipper, two crew members, passenger and dog was merrily on its way downstream on a receding tide. Moore, who was still sleeping in the station wagon, was due to meet the *Sea Swallow* and its crew at Bodega Bay. This was a convenient arrangement to have a vehicle at their disposal.

It was not long before Tod and Johannesen were aroused from their sleeping bags and joined the Colonel and Rolf in the wheelhouse. Passing a beached four-stack destroyer off the port, Johannesen made a general inquiry, "Are we underway?" Then he thought to himself at the sight of Rolf, "Oh, no! Are you coming along?" And then he asked just that.

"Who? Me? No! No!"

The Colonel was keeping the *Sea Swallow* on the western side of the Napa River because of a sunken wooden hay barge near the eastern bank, revealing itself only at the lowest of tides, and known to have ripped out the bottom of the sturdiest of boats. It was at this time when the Colonel was thinking of times past, of his thirty-year army career spanning three wars. Without any formal instruction and/or training, after he retired from the military he endeavored to construct a schooner from a thirty-six-foot lifeboat which he picked up at a Navy surplus auction. The entire project proved to be a positive counterpoint; from a terrestrial army career to a nautical avocation. He had to find and procure the deck plating, lumber, masts, booms, stays, turnbuckles, sails, chocks, cleats, bits, auxiliary engine and transmission, the steering unit, magnetic compass, the electricians and welders…

Looking across the stern of the schooner and its wake, the First Mate asked the Colonel, "Where's the rowboat?"

"We've got the rubber life raft in the forward hold."

"Moore said he ain't getting into that shark trap again."

The statement creased Rolf's forehead as his eyebrows lifted a few centimeters.

"What do you suggest?" asked the Colonel.

"Tony has a rowboat," thought Johannesen out loud.

"You don't want that," advised Rolf. "He put this big motor on it and half the transom fell off. Old Mare Island dock boat."

"Who do you think sold him that boat? The tule fairy?"

"Ah hah! So you're the one who's been peddling off other peoples' boats. It rows pretty good. Heavy as a rock. You might be able to use it. Piece of junk. Tony won't like you taking it, though. That's his baby, you know."

"Well we'll come up with something, or else the raft will have to do," said the Colonel.

Sailing past Napa Slough, Russ Island and finally South Slough, while Might Island and groves of tule reeds were off the port side, Rolf commented that Colonel Rex had some rowboats.

"Colonel Rex?" asked the Colonel.

"Out of the Army Air Corps," answered Tod. "When we were in high school we used to rent boats from him. He can be reasonable. Got to watch out for his dogs though." He gave a hard look at Johannesen, who was a hopeless dog lover and had in fact inadvertently assisted his mongrel aboard. The dog had been waiting for his master outside the barroom when the Sorceress' mad-scene took place, and the mixed-breed dog took flight. Some hours later, not being able to locate his master that night around the outside of the barroom and porch, the dog tracked down Johannesen's scent, boarded the schooner, and entered the cabin by prying open the loosely closed door after Rolf and the two crew members had stumbled aboard. It then came upon the Colonel that Johannesen's dog had snuck aboard that night.

"Hey, Johannesen," he called, and when he caught the Norwegian's attention he continued, "is your dog aboard?"

"Must've come aboard while we were sleeping."

"We'd better get that rowboat," remarked the Colonel with a picture of his friend Bob Moore in his mind's eye.

"I refuse to set foot on his property," declared Johannesen. "I will not allow him to insult me or my pictures again."

"So he kicked you out of his place too."

As Dutchman Slough approached, Johannesen said, "Aren't we going to go up Dutchman Slough?" Obviously Johannesen was waiving his personal restrictions on the place. The current was so strong coming out of the Slough that all hands thought the *Sea Swallow* had run aground but it had not. The marina on the south bank of Dutchman Slough, like so many of its kind, was in a dilapidated condition. A few pilings and driftwood docks berthed a handsome thirty-six-foot planked cabin cruiser and an old twenty-six-foot cabin cruiser, along with some smaller, lighter craft. But the object of interest here was an old custom-built round-bottom twenty-four-foot sloop that was the sole residence of a hermit who was known to other tidal basin dwellers as "the Abbot," but whose name was Lester.

Johannesen began to inform the crew about the resident who lived in the outlandishly designed craft. "Can you imagine living in cramped quarters like that? I know what they say about me," he spoke in tones as if he were a reasonable person, "but he's got me beat by a mile."

A hatch on the cabin of the twenty-four-foot black-tarred hull, which also had legitimate anti-fouling copper paint on its bottom, opened, and out sprang a spry fellow. He wore a faded blue beret, a weathered face that sported a snow-white beard, a faded multi-colored plaid long-sleeved shirt that was rolled up at the elbows, and a pair of faded denims that was more white than blue was fastened to his waist by a piece of twine placed in the belt slots held together by a square knot. He was wearing a worn-out pair of black army shoes without socks. Lester walked on the dock and waved the *Sea Swallow* to the open berth opposite his sloop. He caught the bow line, but the tide was receding and since the *Sea Swallow* had a five-foot keel, the Colonel did not want to chance getting stuck in the mud. After the engine was turned off Lester began to speak in normal sentences and forthright tones. While Lester was speaking, the crew of the *Sea Swallow* was looking upstream at an old sunken lumber ship on the southern bank of Dutchman Slough.

"I would like to invite you onto the dock," stated Lester, "but I am not authorized to do so, so I suggest that you remain aboard."

Examining the two davits and the commercial fishing hand winches on the davits on both sides of the schooner's stern, Lester inquired, "What is your destination?"

"Up the coast," answered the Colonel. The crew and passenger of the *Sea Swallow* were examining Lester's attire, his sloop and the general area, and were only half listening to the conversation between him and the Colonel.

"It has been some time since I made it up the coast, but I have taken my sloop," he referred to it with his right hand, "from Mexico to Canada."

When the meaning of Lester's last statement registered, Johannesen and Tod shot out in unison, "In that?"

"I don't have the accommodations that your boat has, but it is sufficient for my needs," was the explanation.

"You mean to tell us that you have taken *this* boat to Mexico and back?" asked Rolf.

Lester nodded, "Yes. On the return voyage up the coast I lost the southern wind less than a day's sail past Point Conception and had to tack the rest of the way to San Francisco."

"They tell me there's nothing new under the sun, but this has got to be a new one," commented Rolf.

"Does your journey have any particular waypoints?" asked Lester.

"We'd like to make it up the coast as far as Eureka or Crescent City, but probably we'll only make it to Bodega Bay."

Lester moved his head in acknowledgment. He then asked, "What type of navigation instruments do you have? A satellite navigator or a G.P.S.?'"

"We have a magnetic compass, charts and dividers." Looking around, the Colonel explained, "We keep on losing the pencils." He continued, "We'd like to spend some time at Drake's Bay. Have you been there?"

"Most certainly! In fact, on my return trip down the coast some years ago, I stopped over at Drake's Bay. The area there has many edible species of crustaceans. In fact, the place enchanted me to such an extent that I spent ten days there." It was now Lester's turn to inquire, and he hinted, "I heard your internal combustion diesel engine in my bunk and had the feeling you were wanting to stop by."

"Would you like to come aboard and look around?" asked the Colonel.

"It is not my intention to impose upon you."

"Not at all! Would you like a fresh cup of coffee?"

"That I would."

"Where's Ol' Man Rex at?" asked Tod, as he and Johannesen were helping Lester aboard.

"I believe he is away at the moment. Do you require his presence?"

Johannesen answered for everyone, "No, not really."

"This is an interesting place," observed the Colonel. "Would anyone mind if I looked around?"

"If you must, it will have to be at your own risk. Sightseeing is frowned upon by the management." Rolf, Johannesen and Tod were stretching their necks to see if the property owner was hiding behind the jasmine bushes and the tule reeds wielding a sizable artillery piece.

"*Cave canem.*"

"What does that mean," asked the Colonel.

"Beware of the dog," was the answer. Lester confirmed this with an acknowledging grimace, and with this information the Colonel flopped on the dock and was off on his excursion, alone because the other personnel on the schooner knew the place and what he was about to happen upon.

"Commercial fishing, you say," commented Lester. "Have they put into effect the restraints on commercial fishing licenses yet?"

With the ritualistic pot of coffee percolating on the alcohol stove, Lester informed, "I gave up on making my own coffee some years ago. Haven't the medical reports indicated that caffeine debilitates the central nervous system? But I suppose a cup of coffee with milk will not result in any significant neurological damage."

Already the driftwood dock was resting on the bank's mud, and the Colonel was past the tules and jasmine bushes, jogging past a group of shacks off his right shoulder and a 1949 Ford coupe that was hand-painted a bland blue on its forward sections. The winding dirt road led to where the Colonel could see more buildings off to his left; a house elevated on blocks, a line of rowboats filled with dirt serving as big pots in which someone was growing a vegetable garden next to the entrance road from Highway 37, some more buildings to the left, including a storage shed and a small barroom. But what really caught the Colonel's immediate attention were the three bulldogs that were preparing to create a trail of dust in his direction.

"Oh," and the Colonel blurted out a short word synonymous with fertilizer and manure. He reversed his direction back to the docks at Dutchman Slough with the velocity of a high-school track sprinter. The Colonel only hoped to reach the docks before the dogs, because if bad came to worse the *Sea Swallow*'s skipper would jump into the water. No matter how ferocious a canine may be, it is next to harmless in the water. Although the bulldogs were not nipping at his heels just yet, the Colonel had built up so much momentum that he could not turn it off like a water spigot. He went sailing into the muddy water with a splash that was heard inside the *Sea Swallow*.

By the time the occupants of the schooner made it to the deck to see what the latest unscheduled activity was about, the three bulldogs were at the dock's edge, dutifully watching the schooner's occupants pull the skipper aboard with a deck line. Soaking wet on the deck, the Colonel asked, "What was that expression?"

"*Cave canem.*"

"I've got to remember that."

Johannesen's mongrel was on the schooner's deck full of fight, which attracted the astute gaze of the three bulldogs, and for his own safety the mixed-breed hound promptly landed in the forward hold of the cabin via the forward hatch.

"Where is the home port of the *Sea Swallow*?"

"Breezy's."

"About eight miles upriver."

"Breezy's. I've been up that way. But it usually takes me two to three days to make it back. Do I have an auxiliary? I have a 1920 one-cylinder model, a Hicks...correct...with the large flywheel ....Takes me where I need to go. Outboards! Pollute the water. Never could keep up with the spark plug repair. There is no need to be in haste. Where the sails can't take me, I use the auxiliary or an oar." While Lester was speaking, the schooner's crew and visitor were trying to calculate his elusive character. "...Like duck hunters and people who come to the bar to drink alcoholic beverages. They are a vexation to the spirit. Is there any drinking of alcoholic beverages at Breezy's?"

"And I thought I knew everybody on this river," thought Johannesen.

Nothing progressive was being accomplished here. The schooner's bow was resting on the mud, and within five minutes the *Sea Swallow* was on its way out of Dutchman Slough. The Colonel, in a fresh set of clothes, and the crew were ready to forego the acquiring of the rowboat until they moved alongside a cabin cruiser at Vallejo Boat Center to let Rolf off and the people on the schooner had a good view of Tony's green skiff with a quickly but sufficiently repaired transom.

"You should've seen the last boat he had. A square bow scow he picked up at Dowrelio's [a marina on the Carquinez Straits]. It sank here and the tide brought it to the Fishing Bridge, just upstream—north of Vallejo Boat Center," informed Rolf.

As the people were viewing the fifteen-foot, nine-inch heavy-planked double-bottom skiff with two sets of oars, an extra paddle and numerous oversized oarlocks, the needle-nosed skiff that had a stern that flared upward which allowed the skiff to row easily through the water, ideal for their needs, contrary to a straight flat-bottom skiff that drags through the water, Johannesen noticed, "Where's the outboard motor?"

"It's in the repair shop," said Rolf. "Tony and a bunch of his friends took it off last weekend." Then, addressing Tod, "Weren't you with them?"

"Colonel, I'll tell you what," stated Tod, "at first I didn't know who they were talking about, but I know Tony real well. In fact, I helped him take the motor off. Some of us came back and helped him with the rear end." Tod then began to explain the known history of the boat and that it had probably never been more than a few miles from where it was built.

"If only it could talk," was a remark.

Since Tod was part of the "inner circle" of the rowboat club he had permission to take the boat—minus outboard engine—anywhere he wished. "This is as good a time as any," said Tod as he sprang from the schooner to the makeshift wooden dock.

Untying the skiff, Rolf warned Tod as if he was upholding righteousness, "He ain't going to like this."

Johannesen's mystic tidal basin knowledge began to alarm him. "Colonel, I cannot go along with this. The boat has been part of the scenery for the last fifty years. I can just see Ol' Man Smith [the skiff's previous, now-deceased, owner] rowing it with his straw hat on. He wouldn't like this either. Ask anybody from here."

Tod knew that Johannesen had found a legitimate cause to perpetuate his ceaseless complaining. "Colonel, I'll take full responsibility for this. When we get to Bodega Bay I'll give Tony a telephone call and invite him to join us."

The First Mate was closely watching Tod secure the bow line from the skiff that would be the tow line to the schooner.

Johannesen was not going to say anything about how the tow line should be rigged since he did not approve of taking the skiff, but when Tod began to use a single nylon parachute cord, Johannesen could not help but advise, "You'd better make that double," since a single line would be strong enough to tow the small boat, but a single line could more easily chafe apart in the wave action they were sure to pass through.

"Are you sure you know what you're doing?" inquired the heavyset man who was also on the dock observing Tod.

"I suppose."

Tod made a series of granny knots and finally, as Johannesen was still looking on, accidentally made a couple of half-hitches on a steel ring connected to the bowsprit. The Norwegian asked, "Where did you learn to do that?"

"Around here," was the reply.

"I wouldn't brag about it."

With Rolf on the dock shaking his corpulent head disparagingly at the *Sea Swallow* and the skiff on a short tow line, the Colonel took the bugle-like fog horn to his mouth and made a horrendous goose-like sound to signal the drawbridge to open. Johannesen, feeling that only he could blow the fog horn better than anyone else, informed the skipper while taking the fog horn away, "Colonel, there's only one way to blow a fog horn." The native of Norway took a deep breath that crammed his neck between his shoulders and blew into the signal apparatus with eyes bulging, cheeks inflated, and face turning shades of red and blue. After five minutes of this fog horn solo performance, the Mare Island causeway drawbridge finally opened, allowing the *Sea Swallow* to proceed downstream toward the Carquinez Straits. Chug-a-lugging past the Carquinez Straits and the granite rock pile jetties that Johannesen and Fusco had passed in the twenty-six-foot wooden whaleboat sloop *IF* only to drift into the mud flats of the San Pablo Bay some ten years earlier, the *Sea Swallow* crew debated whether or not to hoist a few sails to assist the diesel engine. It was then decided to put the storm jib up and to let out enough line so the rowboat off the stern could roll and pitch on its own seventy-five feet astern of the schooner, where the double nylon cord would stretch out and contract.

The *Sea Swallow*, named after a swallow that had built her nest on the bow while the schooner was under construction, chugged right along. Now, there was never a true seafaring man who would tempt the fates by evicting the swallow or destroying her nest; it was accepted as a bountiful omen, and all concerned settled down to wait with all the eager anticipation of an expectant father. There was much rejoicing and not a little celebrating when two tiny nestlings were hatched. Hence the schooner proudly bore a hand-wrought metal *Sea Swallow* on her bow, which served a dual purpose: first, it added to her grace and beauty; second, a real surprise bonus totally unexpected, no seagull would come near the boat. Evidently the metal image on the bow looked like a bird of prey, and seagulls maintained a safe distance, thus eliminating the constant harassment of raining guano and the consequent cleanup. As a warning device in heavy fog, she sported a lovely bell on the main mast that had once been part of a very old fire truck. Although her hull was totally constructed of metal she had the appearance of being a wooden vessel due to the artistry and talent with the paint brush by the First Mate, Elling Johannesen.

PART TWO

The California Coast

IN THE SANCTUARY OF RACCOON STRAITS, between Angel Island to the port and Tiburon and Sausalito to the starboard, the crew agreed to leave the storm jib up but to slow the diesel engine and pull in the double nylon parachute line. Johannesen volunteered to pull in the rowboat with his dog's approval, but his nicotine-stained lungs began to labor under the strain, and so commenced his grumblings. The rowboat had enough water in it from the wave splash from San Pablo Bay to cause concern, and Johannesen began to complain about this too.

"I told you we'd lose it. Look at all that water. We might as well cut it loose right now."

Tod was thinking, "What is he talking about? The rowboat's in good shape."

"I'll bail it out, Colonel," offered Tod out loud.

"The gods won't like you going against my word," cautioned the Norwegian to Tod and the Colonel.

"Would you get me something so that I can bail this boat out?"

For many men and women, a cup of coffee is essential to guarantee a successful day, and sitting up in a sleeping bag holding his head in the extended interior of his station wagon was not leading to anything in connection with the day's planned activities. In the barroom the aromatic brown beverage prepared from crushed, roasted bean-like seeds was brewing, and after three cups Bob Moore returned to his station wagon, started up the engine and departed for Bodega Bay. On Milton and Los Amigos roads, Moore was passing Napa River bank levee dwellings and slow-growing, small-leafed but corona-shaped California oak trees. The

electrician-musician crossed the narrow concrete bridge over
Carneros Creek that leads to Cuttings Wharf Road, which leads to
Highway 121, where Moore passed vineyards with air-circulating,
frost-preventing airplane engines and propellers—a few fruit or-
chards, walnut groves, cow pastures and areas where the road is
flanked by mighty shadow-casting eucalyptus trees. Once on
Highway 121, Moore passed through the moistureless hills with
the sweet smell of hay that led to Highway 116 to 101, where, at
Petaluma, he entered Stony Point Road, which leads to Roblar
Road which turns into Petaluma Valley Ford, which is the incom-
parable winding Highway One that hugs the breathtaking cliffs
and wooded view of the Pacific Coast that is the route to the mist-
shrouded Bodega Bay, where the hills are verdant from the constant Pacific Ocean moisture.

As the *Sea Swallow* passed under the giant red trademark steel
structure bridging San Francisco County and Marin County with
the little rowboat under tow, the short, choppy waves gave way to
majestic ground swells of the appropriately named Pacific Ocean
that sent the *Sea Swallow* surging as the crew witnessed the
Creator's composition in motion, the endless following of ground
swells that eventually crash into the cliffs of Point Bonita, Point
Diablo, or break down into smaller waves in the San Francisco Bay
or become the surf on a sandy beach.

After looking astern and seeing that the rowboat was riding
the six-to-eight-foot swells much better than the choppy waves of
the inland bay water, Tod thought to himself, "Tony would be
proud of how his boat is handling. Bet he never dreamed his boat
would make it out here."

Just then Johannesen commented, "Colonel, this is as good a
time as any to cut the boat loose."

After looking astern and seeing that the rowboat was handling
itself very well, the Colonel remarked, "She's doing all right. If
anything has to be done, we'll get it."

"Okay, Colonel. Anything you say. But if anything happens," he added, giving a reproving finger, "don't blame me."

Looking straight at Johannesen with one of the many verbal reprimands the First Mate was to receive during the trip, Tod thought, "How did that hermit put it? Oh, yeah. 'Vexation of the spirit.'"

Johannesen clutched his dog, instructing him, "Watch him, dog, watch him," and the dog obeyed his master's command.

It was unanimously decided to hoist all of the sails on the *Sea Swallow*. The outer jib, also known as the storm jib, was already raised, and to join it came the inner jib. The *Sea Swallow* was as rustic as it was stout. There were no fancy tracks and winches to shift and secure the jib sails. A person had to tightly grab the line at the end of the jib and secure it to a cleat, a railing post, or whatever appeared to be handy at the moment. If the line whipped out of a person's hand, this made the detail that much more aggravating, trying to catch the snaking line as it slapped one senseless in the face as the dacron sails wildly clapped in the wind. The reef points loosened the halyards, raising the main and mizzen sheets, and secured to a cleat on the main and mizzen mast; the *Sea Swallow* was under full sail as the Colonel shut down the diesel engine, tacking to the northeast for about forty-five minutes, then to the northwest for twenty minutes. As the schooner neared Point Reyes, the fog as usual began to set in, and Johannesen began his familiar dirge:

"It's an omen from the gods. I remember U-boat sailors talked about weather like this. Anything can happen."

The Colonel, smiling, was taking this dialogue in stride. "Look! We can't even see the rowboat. That old man who owned that boat is putting a curse on us. And that Lester. He's around here—somewhere." He looked around as if Lester were about to sail out of the fog and into view. "And wanting to know where we were going. And he was interested in our navigational devices, too."

Though it was summer, the fog gave a wintry impression that made Tod remember a painting Johannesen had agreed to paint some years earlier for a friend—Stephen—and wanted to know if it had been completed. Tod's last recollection was that it had not been.

"Johannesen, do you remember a painting you were supposed to make for Stephen?" Johannesen did not want to answer, and Tod continued, "He told me you only made the sketch."

Johannesen finally spoke up. "I had the outline done and would have completed it, but Fusco came over, it was Christmas, and we went to Tom's house." The Norwegian continued that it had been cold and he had not wanted to spend Christmas alone in the houseboat in which he was living at the time. What Johannesen omitted was that on Christmas Eve he had been at a waterfront bar party, where Stephen had located him and asked about the painting. The patrons and the bar owner thought he had swindled the boy, and he was escorted out. He fell asleep behind the building on a pile of eucalyptus leaves, where some people from the Salvation Army found him. "You know, I almost finished the picture; I was almost done when I went out, and when I came back it was gone."

"He really wanted to have that painting for his parents."

"That was some time ago. You still remember."

"Do you have a knife handy?"

"Not on me."

Tod shrugged, "Nevermind," then he asked the Colonel, "Would it be all right if I go in the cabin and read? You don't need any help with the wheel, do you?"

"Go right ahead. Johannesen and I can handle this."

"He sure can get moody—and for no reason. Colonel, do you think we should keep the rowboat?"

"I'll make a deal with you," offered the Colonel. "We'll let the rowboat alone, we'll leave the line where it's at." He indicated the stern cleat where the nylon cord had been made fast with numerous figure eights. "If the gods wish to take the boat, they can have it. If not, we'll simply keep it."

Johannesen agreed. It would have been an insult to Odin and the rest of his brothers, cousins, and other related deities if Johannesen believed what the Colonel was insinuating, that the gods were incapable of taking the fog-bound rowboat at will.

Inside the schooner's cabin Tod came in direct contact with Johannesen's dog, and the only thing to do was try to make friends with the animal, which the young man proceeded to do rather unconvincingly. The dog perceived this and vacated the cabin to the deck, where his master was at the wheel.

At this moment Johannesen sounded the call—a call all too familiar to sailors on and off watch.

"All hands on deck."

"What's it this time, Johannesen?"

"We're in irons! Irons! All hands on deck!"

"Irons?" thought Tod. In his mind's eye he could see a large ship bearing down on the *Sea Swallow* with its bow wave and anchor and heavy chain dangling in a menacing manner.

On his feet and on the main deck following Johannesen, Tod was looking around for the ship when the Colonel explained, "The wind died down and we have to bring in the sails."

The native of Norway put his complaining nature aside as he commanded the reefing of the sails. The Colonel was cranking up the Budda diesel. But this cooperation could not last long. As soon as the Colonel had finished lighting off the Budda engine, Johannesen was exclaiming, "Colonel! Colonel! How soon are we going to be at Bodega Bay? We're out of cigarettes." The Colonel did not smoke nor indulge in more than two glasses of anything alcoholic during an evening.

"Can you hold out until dark?"

Since the *Sea Swallow* no longer had to tack, everybody was looking forward to entering Bodega Bay. The schooner would arrive early enough for the crew to relax and share yarns of every de-

scription in the many smoke-filled barrooms situated at the popular fishermen's haven.

Returning fully to his original form when it came time to haul
in the rowboat close aboard, Johannesen would not take any
physical part in the chore. Instead he stood back and continued his
mistrustful talk about the rowboat.

"You know, the Coast Guard can cite us for having this boat.
It doesn't have any C.F. numbers. We don't have any towing sig-
nals. It don't got no lights."

Johannesen continued his moaning while dropping the anchor
in the southern end of Bodega Bay near the first fish shed off
Highway 1, and once again some aspects of his complaining were
not unfounded. "Damn, this anchor is heavy! You know, we should
have a winch to raise this." Tod agreed.

"Wonders never cease. They finally got a rowboat," said
Moore out loud. Johannesen was rowing the Colonel, Tod, the dog
and himself to where Moore was waiting on the dock, and the
Norwegian refused any help.

"No, I'll do it myself."

The Colonel was of no humor and wanted to be dockside. He
rinsed himself off from the salt water swim earlier in the day and
wanted to take a legitimate shower somewhere on shore.

Sitting on a bar stool with his guitar, Moore began to sing one
of his ballads:

Oh, lonely is lonely
How lonely we be
We fought and we died
To keep you free.
Oh, my friend,
Do you know what it is to lie
Beneath a powder blue sky.

"Your friend sings a very touching melody."

"He's part of the crew. I'm Johannesen, first mate of the *Sea Swallow.*" He offered his hand to reinforce the introduction. "Which boat are you from?"

"My boat is that white one over there." The sun had set as he pointed through a large picture window facing west to an anchored former military vessel readapted for fishing that was illuminated by a bright lantern on the aft deck.

"Then you must be a Captain."

The part-time commercial fisherman with an elegantly styled silver beard shrugged, "If you want to put it that way."

"Captain," offered Johannesen, "let me offer you a drink for good luck and to the gods." This statement produced a slightly off-beat look from the silver-haired fisherman.

Tod was thinking, "What is this river rat up to?"

"Waiter! Waiter!" accosted Johannesen at an exclusive bar counter. "Would you please attend to this man and myself?" Catching a glimpse of Tod, he added, "and him, too." Three minutes later Tod had to help subsidize Johannesen's generosity. Involved in the caper, Tod was closely following the proceedings.

"If I may ask, how do you transport yourself from your boat to the dock?"

"Through the auspices of an eight-foot aluminum dinghy," was the answer.

"Is that how a Captain should transport himself?"

"Since you mentioned it, no."

"I'll offer you a proposal. We have this rowboat...."

Bob Moore was thinking, "Up to one of his shenanigans—again?"

"...that after we leave here we'll have little use for. Would you care to pick it up?"

"How much are you asking?"

"We will let it go for, let's say, for the price of the oars and the oarlocks."

"And what's that?"

"Thirty-five, forty dollars."

"Thirty dollars."

"Sold!"

Johannesen was almost knocked over by a direct kick from one of his fellow crew members who was mentally screaming, "You can't do that!"

Johannesen then gave the crew member a subtle look of reassurance and worded "watch" with his mouth.

The silver-bearded fisherman was digging into his left back pocket for his wallet to get the legal notes of tender for all debts, public and private, with reproduced portraits of Presidents Jackson, Lincoln and Washington on their front sides to pay for the item he had just bargained for. When he handed the money over to Johannesen, the First Mate informed him, "It's the green rowboat with the two sets of oars and big—real big—oarlocks," demonstrating with his hands. "You can't miss it. It's got no C.F. numbers. It's at the small boat dock."

"When are you leaving?"

"In a couple of days."

"Just so we know where to find it."

The new owner of the rowboat purchased a fresh round of drinks to formally celebrate the transaction as Johannesen began to extol the fifteen-foot, nine-inch boat's attributes. "It's a heavy rowboat—double bottom. Made to be rowed. Don't make 'em like that anymore. Even has two coats of bottom paint on it." Turning to Tod, Johannesen added, "Tony always pampered that boat too much." Tod was too dumbfounded to respond to anything.

Recovering his senses, Tod decided it would be best to call the real owner of the rowboat. Outside by the coin-operated telephones, numerous cats with splendid fur coats attained by the scraps from the fish sheds that protected the animals from the perpetual cold night fog were wandering about.

He placed a quarter in the telephone, heard the blank dial tone, dialed one, then the area code, then the number; the operator signaled, "Seventy-five cents, please."

Three copper-based Washington-head quarters were promptly placed in the telephone coin slot. A few seconds later the telephone receiver was vibrating with, "What did you do with my boat?"

"We got it up here at Bodega Bay."

"Did it make it?"

"Of course! What do you think we did, lose it?" Nothing was said about Johannesen's premonitions concerning the gods and the boat, nor about the latest financial transaction. Instead Tod said, "Rode the seas out great. Should've seen it."

"When am I going to get it back?"

After a moment of thought, Tod answered, "It'll be no problem to tow it back. People tow dinghies all the time. We're going to be leaving soon to somewhere...."

"Where?"

"Somewhere around the coast."

"Point Reyes?"

"Yeah. Drake's Bay."

He vaguely remembered the name from somewhere.

"I ought to make it up there this weekend."

This was Tod's original design, but as circumstances developed he thought that it would be wiser to implement a change of plan.

"Ah, Tony?"

"Yeah."

"I don't think that will be necessary. I'll look after everything. You ought to see all of the cats up here. All kinds of 'em, yellow ones, white ones, there's even a...."

"What boat are you on?" interrupted Tony. "The *Sea Swallow*?... I remember, built up by Breezy's.... Hmmm... Johannesen there?... Should've figured on that... Who else?... Watch that—" employing a series of antonyms of a real trustworthy, reliable fellow. Then in an acquiescent voice, Tony admitted, "It might as well be up there. Wasn't doing much sitting at the dock here."

Not long thereafter, the crew of the *Sea Swallow* piled into the "sold" rowboat, and once again Johannesen insisted on rowing back to the schooner.

On the twenty-four-foot black sloop floating in Dutchman Slough, Lester finished stocking his boat with canned goods, consisting mostly of soup and beans, and had a person in ownership of a vehicle to purchase bread, powdered milk, dry cereal and a few other similar goodies for his voyage influenced by his visit and conversation with the crew of the *Sea Swallow*. A month's supply of fresh water was stored in plastic jugs, along with a month's supply of alcohol for his Coleman stove and lamp and twenty gallons of petrol for his museum-piece auxiliary engine. Lester also had onboard an old government-issue shovel and pick, the original purpose of which was to dig the sloop out of the mud when it ran aground. But Lester was also to bring aboard his sloop a modern electronic mechanism: a hand-operated metal scanner and two rectangular nine-volt dry-cell batteries.

The most logical route from Dutchman Slough to the Pacific Ocean is the direction the *Sea Swallow* took. After leaving the slough eastward, it made an easy ninety-degree starboard turn downstream on the Napa River, passed under the large Highway 37 bridge, passed the drawbridge to the Carquinez Straits, where a starboard turn would be taken in a westerly direction that would eventually lead to the Pacific Ocean. Lester chose another peculiarly interesting and scenic route. Instead of entering the Napa River and passing under the big Highway 37 bridge, Lester went up Dutchman Slough, west-northwest and sometimes due north, as the tide had been flooding the tidal basin for about two hours. With a small auxiliary engine and the five-foot draft of his boat, Lester had to be careful in the narrow Dutchman Slough, but he had calculated correctly. He would have the tide in his favor, winding through the slough into South Slough as he passed on his port side some farmland on which some city and county officials and land developers would construct a coterie waterfront community and salt beds to his starboard. Once Lester and his custom-built sloop putt-putted into Napa Slough, the tide would be receding, assisting him past a naval reservation to his starboard, because the water in the slough would be flowing out of the nearest entrance, Sonoma Creek, rather than the entrances of Dutchman Slough and South Slough, which are many more miles away. Lester anticipated that he would most probably run aground and that at low tides these sloughs would become impassable even to the shallowest-draft skiff, and that it could take fifteen hours just to get to San Pablo Bay by way of Sonoma Creek, passing under a moderate-size bridge there. The recluse even surprised himself when, twelve hours later that evening, he was out of the narrow and shallow channel and stuck in the mud by Tubbs Island, taking the delay as standard procedure and occupying himself preparing supper.

After a breakfast of bread, peanut butter and jelly, milk and of course the hallowed coffee and cigarettes, the crew of the *Sea Swallow* was ready to set out for their initial serious day of commercial fishing. The "sold" rowboat hung off of its own anchor, and the schooner's anchor was heaved. With the usual bickering the *Sea Swallow* was soon on its way sailing past Campbell Cove, swinging north of Bodega Rock and straight for the open sea in a west-southwest direction. It was a foggy gray morning, and for the first three miles there were runabouts and rowboats at anchor, and in them were men, women and children bundled up in winter clothes with angles in the water. Past the three-mile point from the coast, the *Sea Swallow* found itself only in company with large commercial fishing boats. As one girdie, or small hand-winch, on a davit containing stainless steel cable with snap attachments held in place by brass stoppers that hold swivels, leaders and fishing lures with a lump of lead at the end of the cable, could be paced out, the sea began to mount to such a height that in the intervals between waves the other fishing boats could not be seen. It is at times like this that an experienced seaman such as Johannesen foresees that someone is about to become seasick. In fact, Johannesen was steering the *Sea Swallow* in the waves just to induce this unwelcome feeling in one of the crew members. Tod tapped Johannesen on the shoulder and said, "I'll take the wheel for a while," in very pale tones.

Tod was in no physical condition to hold the wheel, and Johannesen knew it; but the youngest crew member was insistent, and against his better judgment the Norwegian relinquished the helm. Tod reasoned that if he occupied his mind, it would distract him from the awful feeling of losing his equilibrium. The schooner was pitching so much it was difficult for Johannesen to hold a magnetic compass course, since the compass was shifting fifteen degrees with every other wave. The wheel required some strength to hold, and Tod was having trouble distinguishing where the sea ended and the sky began. Johannesen and Moore had a delightful time watching Tod struggle, until finally the Norwegian came to Tod's rescue and took over the wheel, with no objection from the younger man. The Colonel had felt the effects of the sea, too, but he rebounded after a few minutes and was eating a baked potato. Seeing the Colonel eating something, Tod took a closer look, and the Colonel offered, "Tod! You're as white as a sheet. Here, have a potato."

Tod had drunk some beer and three glasses of hot water and brandy with a lemon twist the night before, and he felt like an entire fifth of whiskey was about to erupt from within himself. The once-pleasing aroma of brandy now merged with that downright miserable feeling of being seasick. Tod was thinking, "Maybe the Colonel is right. If I eat some potatoes, I'll feel better."

"Let me have a potato."

"A whole one, or a half one?"

"I'll take that one." He pointed to a large half baked potato wrapped in aluminum foil.

"Put some salt on it. It will make you feel better," offered the Colonel. "Anytime I feel something coming on, I just eat a little and it goes away."

Taking the Colonel's advice, Tod put liberal quantities of salt on his half-potato and began to gobble away at the starchy tuber. For a while he thought it was doing some good. Tod looked at Johannesen and Moore, who had easily drunk three times as much alcohol as himself, and they were not seasick in the least. Then it happened. Everything hit at once. There was no end to the *Sea Swallow*'s constant motion in the steady twelve-foot seas. Tod was smelling beer, brandy, potatoes and salt all at once. He lay down in the cabin, where Johannesen's dog was in not so good shape either, and glued his eyes to the overhead, but this did not do any good either. He was completely without balance, and he simply wanted to take the necessary steps to get over it. On the port stern quarter of the schooner he vomited, and when parts of the vomit went back down his throat threatening to choke him, in his disgust he stamped his foot and the whole lousy mess came coughing out.

Moore and Johannesen were choking too, but with laughter. Tod was so mad that he would have thrown both of them overboard if he had had the strength. Tod was so out of it that the Colonel had to stop eating his potato and hold on to him to make sure he did not fall overboard. When Tod's vomiting act was concluded, the Colonel had to get a bucket with a line attached to the handle, put it overboard, and haul up water to wash the deck where Tod was standing.

"He'll never make it!" roared Johannesen.

"I don't mean to make fun of you," said Moore, "but you—you were a sight, stomping your feet." He imitated the motion. "Should've seen the look on your face!" The laughter continued.

Feeling somewhat better, Tod tapped Johannesen once more on the shoulder, but the *Sea Swallow* was maneuvering between other fishing boats, and with the waves blocking the view of the other boats and their trolling cables, Johannesen explained why he should remain at the wheel.

It was rough, and the *Sea Swallow* was not catching anything; by observing other fishing boats with binoculars, it was known that they, too, were not bringing in any salmon. So, since everyone had to hold on to a fixed object so as not to fall down, it was decided to reel in the trolling cable, take off the snap-attached lures and hooks, and return to the coast and try for bottom fish in a sheltered cove. Was Tod happy to learn about the change of plans! The odd thing about the waves was that there was little wind, and the fog still hovered a few hundred feet above the water. Once the coast came into sight the waves began to simmer down, and just south of Horseshoe Cove, where the *Sea Swallow* anchored, the water turned mirror-calm and the sun began to burn away the fog.

Within half an hour fishing poles and drop lines were cast from the schooner, their hooks supporting anchovy bait. Johannesen and Moore were surprised to see how quickly Tod had revived from his motion sickness, and once again the Norwegian found a cause to complain.

"Colonel! He's eating everything he can get his hands on. It'll be our luck to run out of stores in the middle of the week. We're gonna have to go ashore tonight."

"Johannesen. Check your pole. I think you've got something."

The Norwegian began to fight with the fishing pole, and wild ideas of what might be on the end of the line entered the crew members' thoughts. Whatever was on the end of the hook, it was large enough to move the *Sea Swallow* on its anchor line.

"Get the net! I don't want to lose it!" ordered Johannesen.

Tod got the catch net, which looked large enough to bag Moby Dick. The Colonel and Tod were both on their stomachs. Tod was holding on to the end of the pole, and the Colonel was guiding the ring where the net was attached. As the fish came into view and the crew caught a good look at it, it appeared to be a sting ray. When it was finally netted and brought aboard, the crew began to discuss just what had been yanked up from the bottom of the sea.

"Never saw a fish like that before."

"Want to throw it back?"

"This might be the only thing we'll catch."

Johannesen's dog, now up and about, was sniffing around the floundering fish, and it entered the Norwegian's mind that here was a good supply of dogfood. "He might have something—wonder if this fish has a lot of bones?" After consulting a book containing amply drawn illustrations of fish of the Pacific Coast, it was learned that the fish Johannesen had caught was a skate, with only cartilage instead of bones, indicating its antiquated life form which made it ideal victuals for both dog and crew. Under its drawing in the book it simply stated "very edible." The skate weighed out to twenty-two pounds.

Nothing else was caught for the next two hours, and the anchovy bait was being stolen by undersized crabs. The crew, worn out from the previous day's and night's activities and from the high waves of that day, decided to suspend fishing. With the fishing angles reeled in and the drop lines and the boat's anchor raised, the schooner was soon anchored by the green rowboat at the southeast end of Bodega Harbor. On the way into the harbor the skate was cleaned and chopped up for the evening meal.

While on shore to purchase more bread, milk and anchovy bait, the crew of the *Sea Swallow* sat down at a picnic table outside a grocery store and drank some beer. Some tourists with cameras were milling about and began to take pictures of the "hardy fishermen." Johannesen was at his best posing for pictures, nonchalantly sipping beer and conversing in his slightly accented English with the tourists about his experiences. Moore took his guitar out of its black leather case and began to sing one of his ballads, and a small crowd began to form around the crew of the *Sea Swallow*. The people were genuinely being entertained, and when Moore had finished his song the entire crowd, including some other fishermen and his own shipmates, gave him a well-earned round of applause.

That evening Tod cooked part of the skate. He ate more by far than anyone else. Moore flatly refused to eat any of it.

"I don't eat anything I don't know what it is."

The Colonel ate some of the white fish meat, but Johannesen took this opportunity to engage in another round of vocal dissatisfaction. "How did you cook this?"

"I tried to fry it, but I think it got steamed instead."

"Which is it? Did you use any onions?" After tasting a little bit of it, Johannesen said "Put any salt on it?" After eating still a little more, "How do you expect me to eat this when you don't know if it's fried or steamed?" After more nibbling, "No onions...powdered onions....What kind of cook are you, anyway? This could use some garlic too...powdered garlic...should have opened a can of sardines." Johannesen then put his plate on the deck so his dog could eat, and the canine immediately wolfed down the white fish meat.

Early that evening the fog rolled in fast and heavy. It had been quite a day, and the Colonel had planned to turn in early. Johannesen, Moore and Tod took the rowboat ashore for another evening at the bar, leaving the Colonel and the dog behind to hold down the fort, as they say on the *Sea Swallow*. Johannesen's faithful mongrel filled the night air with strains of howling for his departed master until the fog and darkness silently enveloped the rowboat.

"Shouldn't leave my dog like that."

"I don't think they'd let him in the bar. They didn't seem to be pleased with him last night."

"What has my dog done to them? That's what's wrong with the world. People! If people would take after dogs—then we might have something."

Within seconds of entering the barroom, the Norwegian was facing another confrontation brought upon himself by the void *ab initio* business deal he made the night before.

"Johannesen, there's the fellow you sold the boat to. Going to sell him anything else?"

"Don't say anything. He's coming this way."

Moore and Tod waited to see how Johannesen would weave his way out of this one.

"I saw you went fishing today," opened the Norwegian. "How did it go?"

"Got three big ones. Just enough to cover expenses."

"We got a bottom fish. Had to come in early, though. The boy here got seasick out there. You know how it is."

Moore continued, "You should've seen him. Pounding his foot. Never saw anything like it in my life."

The urbane-looking gentleman was looking toward Tod, who was thinking, "Funny. Real funny."

"When are you fellows going to be leaving?"

"Within a day or two. You've seen the rowboat?"

The man nodded, "Yes."

"You'll know where it'll be.…"

About half an hour later Johannesen began expressing his desire to get back to the *Sea Swallow*. Moore was having a grand time drinking vodka straight with a beer chaser and playing requests on his guitar. Not learning from the night before, Tod had finished a beer and now had a glass of hot water and brandy with a lemon twist in front of him.

"I'm going to the boat," informed Johannesen. "You can do what you want."

Convinced that Johannesen was departing and not knowing if they could find another mode of transportation to the *Sea Swallow* other than swimming, they joined the Norwegian. Moore and Tod also knew that Johannesen was about to pull off one of his great escapes from the man to whom he'd 'sold' the rowboat. Not long thereafter all three of them were on the *Sea Swallow* and Johannesen, fearing for his safety, pursued his escape plan.

"Colonel! Colonel!" urged Johannesen to the skipper in his army sleeping bag.

"What is it, Johannesen?"

"We've gotta go! Right now!"

"What are you talking about?"

"A storm is coming. We've got to get to sea!"

After this conversation concluded, the Colonel consented to Johannesen's wish. The diesel engine was lit off, the anchor was raised, and, with the rowboat in tow, the *Sea Swallow*, dripping with dew, was making headway, causing slight ripples in the water in the dense fog. Johannesen was more than willing to assist in getting the schooner under way and did not indulge in his usual complaining.

"Johannesen, I can't see," shouted the Colonel.

The Norwegian went to the bowsprit and began to direct the Colonel where to steer the *Sea Swallow*.

"Starboard! Starboard!" directed the Norwegian.

With hesitation the Colonel followed Johannesen's directions. Then, suddenly, out of the fog on the starboard side came four high-beam lights accompanied by the thunder of a large diesel truck.

"Go to the port! To port! Look out, Colonel! We're going to get hit by a truck. A truck!" Johannesen was running back to where the Colonel was standing by the wheel, and it appeared certain that the truck was going to run over the *Sea Swallow*. But suddenly the schooner hit hard aground on the sandy bottom, knocking everyone off their footing.

"Where do you come from?"

"Norway-Stavanger."

"When was the last time you made it back there?"

"I was going to, but never got around to it."

"I can see why."

Zigzagging up the coast, Lester would call out, "Preparing to come about; coming about! Preparing to jibe; jibing!" Weary after thirty-six hours of constant sailing and tacking with just a brief respite on the mud, the old man decided to drop anchor at the mouth of

Bolinas Lagoon. In short order he had a crab trap placed over the side and a pot of canned soup on the alcohol stove. After supper, Lester settled down by his alcohol lamp and began to leaf through magazines of the latest yacht construction of both power and sail. He chuckled to himself at how the magazines advertised large power boats equipped with hot water tanks, showers and windshield wipers. "They'd like to make this into another trailer park or super freeway, if they could," he thought to himself. Power craft with limited nautical and practical purpose other than generating a sizable wake by indolent members of the suburban class with a little extra money to throw around on the weekend did not hold any esteem to this tidal basin habitant.

Lester took particular interest in the most recent sailboat design and its latest machinery, contrary to his custom-built sloop. A modern sloop, yawl or ketch can sail about twenty-eight degrees into the wind before it has to tack or change direction to maintain some measure of course. If Lester in his sloop or the crew of the *Sea Swallow* attempted this feat, their boats would come to an abrupt halt, then would begin to move at an angle in a reverse direction, the definition of "irons." The wind would then direct the bow head-on, and the sails would flap wildly about.

Lester also had books on various subjects aboard his sloop: books on local folklore, mythology and California history, including magazines on similar topics. Also on board for his reading pleasure were Shakespearean plays, some dated news and sports magazines and yellowed newspapers.

"I've never seen that light so close."

"What do you see now?"

"That light I've been keeping track of. It's on this side of the Saint George's Fishery."

"What's he looking for?"

"Want to go out there and ask him?"

"I wouldn't answer the door if he knocked on it."

"Should we call the park service?"

"They'd probably report us. We could wind up in the Aleutians with Randolph on a buoy tender."

"This is absurd, letting an old man who's got nothing better to do than putter in the dark spook us like—like a bunch of kids in a graveyard. I'd be ashamed if the other watch found out about this. We'd really get transferred then."

Putting on his navy-blue work jacket, the Coast Guard petty officer declared with military resolve, "I'm going to find out just what is going on out here. We're the authorities, you know. Get a report ready, I'm gonna fill it out when I return," and he opened the door and began making his way toward the moving lantern.

By now the light had passed the Coast Guard Station to the south, and the young sailor was having difficulty catching up with the drifting light that seemed to be floating over the many obstacles he was stumbling over. When the sailor found the path to be too dangerous even if it had been daylight—and he had left his flashlight at the station—he thought he should turn back. But then, not conscious of where he was walking, he tripped on some sharp rocks and fell, almost sliding down a steep embankment into the water. The man with the lantern momentarily stopped, looked behind him at his fallen follower, and the young sailor caught a good view of him as he continued on.

"What did you find? Man, you must've fallen; you're dirty." Then the sailor showed his watch partner his abraded hands.

"What happened? What did he do to you?"

"Nothing. He didn't do anything. I fell."

"Gonna fill out a report?"

Signaling with his hand, the sailor took a seat in a chair and shook his head "no" in total consternation.

"Johannesen! How did we let you talk us into this?" mourned Moore on the aft deck of the *Sea Swallow*. "Should've known better. Now we're stuck."

The Colonel, Johannesen and Tod were digging a channel
around the marooned schooner so that she could right herself and
float off more easily when the incoming tide arrived. With this accomplished, the three were digging a line toward the water when a
fishing boat passed as close as it could without running aground,
and somebody yelled for the Norwegian.

"Johannesen, if I *ever* get my hands on you," yelled the man to
whom the first mate had sold the rowboat, "I'm going to crown
you with one of those oars."

"What's this all about?" asked the Colonel, who was up to his
knees in mud with an army surplus shovel.

"Nothing much," dismissed Johannesen. "I sold him some
merchandise a while back and he seems to be a little dissatisfied."

"How could we have let him talk us into this?" continued
Moore. "Colonel, as soon as we're free I'm going to drive my car
home."

"What can I say, Bob?" was the reply. "Suit yourself. We
should be free by the next high tide."

"The last high tide didn't even float the rowboat."

"There's going to be a seven-foot tide in twelve hours."

"*Twelve hours*! Johannesen, stay away from me. I'm not responsible from here on out for what I'm liable to do to you."
Brooding in the cabin of the *Sea Swallow,* Moore came upon the
adventure magazine that Tod had purchased and began to file
through it himself.

GOLD IN THEM THAR HILLS, declared one headline. "Sounds like
the time the Colonel and I went prospecting in Mexico," thought
Moore.

CALIFORNIA GOLD MINING, read another article.

TREASURE HUNTING TIPS.

WHAT TO TAKE, WHAT NOT TO TAKE.

WHAT TO DO. WHAT NOT TO DO.

DID GERONIMO BURY HIS FORTUNE—WHERE?

An article on ghosts in a valley caught the musician poet's passing eye, and he read the entire tale. The article was well written and documented, and Moore retracted his initial opinion that the periodical was nothing more than a cheap, get-rich-quick publication. The entire magazine began to intrigue Moore, and in the table of contents he found an article on Drake's Bay.

The Colonel, Johannesen and Tod were still keeping themselves occupied digging the hurried channel for the *Sea Swallow*, and Moore could easily hear their conversation through the metal hull.

"You think he's going to leave?"

"He might."

Moore heard sounds of shovels against mud and small seashells, then the flat sounds of mud and shells being flung and splattered a few feet away.

"You never know what he's going to do. He should get over it."

"Before the water comes up we will have to get the anchor out over there." The Colonel pointed to the direction of the water.

The article in the adventure magazine about Sir Francis Drake and his namesake body of water was like the other articles. Although somewhat far-fetched for total credibility, it was very well written and well documented, complete with photographs of the bay and of an important related artifact. The published essay left the lingering question: What did Drake do with his treasure, which was unaccounted for in England?

Having finished reading the article, Moore made it to the deck by the main mast to see the progress of the incoming tide, and the guitarist asked the Colonel, "Where are you going when we get floated?"

"We've decided to try our luck at Drake's Bay. Not much going on around here except for the nightlife." He pointed toward the barrooms, stores and motels of Bodega Bay.

Johannesen confirmed this with an agreeing, "That's for sure."

"There isn't a bar within twenty miles of Drake's Bay," continued the Colonel. "That ought to keep us straight."

"I'll meet you over there. I'm taking my station wagon."

The rest of the crew was glad that Moore was having a change of heart about the events that were beyond his control, even though they did not know what was responsible for his change in mood. Still, Moore did not trust the crew member with the shocks of unruly blond hair. In fact, he did not even trust the voyage itself. But he was willing to see just what was about to happen.

Everyone came aboard, the dog sat on the stern of the boat wagging his tail amid muddy boots and shovels, and the tide inched forward.

"We're drifting."

"We're afloat!

The anchor strung out on the port side toward deep water; with Tod and Johannesen pulling on the anchor line, the *Sea Swallow* began to kedge itself toward deep water, where her keel would be free of the sand and mud.

—PART THREE—

Drake's Bay

PAST CAMPBELL COVE, SWINGING TO PORT past Bodega Rock, the *Sea Swallow* once again began to ride on the expanding Pacific swells. The organized twelve-foot swells off the starboard quarter that effortlessly placed the *Sea Swallow* atop a wave then in a trough where the schooner would squirm until it would start ascending again were a stark contrast to the jolting cross waves that the schooner had been in the day before. One crew member was relieved that he was feeling no ill effects. "Hey, Johannesen!"

"What do you want?"

"Take the wheel for a minute, would ya?"

When the voyage began Johannesen did not deem Tod worthy to hold the watch. At another time he was too sick to hold a wheel watch. Fully recovered and fitting into life at sea, Tod now held sixty percent of the wheel watch. Within half an hour Johannesen had Tod back on the wheel, and the Norwegian was sitting on a milk crate with a lost expression on his face.

"Johannesen! What's wrong?" asked Tod.

"Don't feel well."

"Don't tell me you're seasick," asked Tod.

"I wish it was that," was the Norwegian's answer.

"Johannesen. You're not seasick are you?" asked the Colonel.

"Seasick! Hah!" responded Johannesen with a snort of the nose and mouth. "I'm not like him," he said, alluding to Tod at the wooden-spiked wheel, getting a moment's relief from a laugh. "My head is killing me," he said, holding his jaw with his right hand.

"Those rotten teeth," thought Tod.

"Come here, Johannesen," offered the Colonel. "I got some aspirin inside."

While searching for the bottle of aspirin in both the wheel-house and the cabin, the fishing lures hooked to the bulkhead in-sulation by the portholes in the wheel house caught the Colonel's attention.

It was agreed that a single salmon lure was to be placed on the trolling cable, on the remote chance that a big fish might be caught. The engine's speed was lowered to 900 revolutions per minute, a trifle high for trolling, but nothing was expected to be caught anyway. It was about this time that Tod was informed that the *Sea Swallow*'s compass was reading thirty degrees off course to the port.

Before sixty minutes had passed, the Colonel thought he saw a big silver fish jump out of the water astern of the schooner in the vicinity of the lure. The engine was slowed down so the steel troll-ing cable could be reeled in by hand, and indeed a large fish had been hooked. But it had gotten away. The evidence was quite ap-parent; the fish was so large that, aided by the high trolling speed, it had bent the barbed hook straight.

Traveling along Highway 1 in his white station wagon, Moore turned west on the winding Sir Francis Drake Boulevard, which leads into the village of Inverness. Here Moore picked up some additional stores for the *Sea Swallow*—cigarettes and some "spirit water" included. On Sir Francis Drake Boulevard, where the road is closest to Drake's Estero Schooner Bay, in the misty haze Moore thought he caught a glimpse of a person in a tall, broad-brimmed sugarloaf hat and a cloak; and although visibility was poor, Moore could see that his attire was worn and his shoes were not like any-thing he had seen before. He was holding a scepter over his left shoulder, which Moore believed to be a stick with a lantern at-tached to it.

"Maybe they're making a movie out here," thought the musi-cian-poet. "Who knows? Looks like a pilgrim." He had read about pilgrims in his junior high school years. The man's back was facing

Moore, but he could see the man had a beard. Then the man walked behind a fog-bound ground slope.

Moore slowed his road-worn white station wagon almost to a standstill at the sight of the "pilgrim," but he did not give it a further thought as he continued on his way along Drake's namesake Boulevard, parallel to Point Reyes Beach, to the west, where Pacific Ocean swells could be heard crashing on the beach, though because of the fog they could not be seen.

Mysteriously, as Bob Moore had entered the fog when leaving Inverness and the Tomales Bay area in his rear-view mirror, he departed the fog mass on the steep downgrade toward Saint George's Fishery on the southeast end of Point Reyes, where fishing boats were placidly anchored and the majority of fishermen were descendants of Calabrese and Sicilian pescatores.

Nursing his decaying teeth, Johannesen notice that his dog was lying near the adventure magazine Tod had picked up. The tenor of the articles, which were close to Johannesen's heart, temporarily relieved the pain in his head.

"Hey, Colonel?"

"What is it, Joe?" said the reassuring voice, answering with a nickname by which the Norwegian was also known.

"I've got something to show you."

Johannesen showed the Colonel the magazine, and he came upon the article on Drake's Bay.

"Look here, Colonel. An article on Drake's Bay."

The Colonel and the Norwegian read the article, and then Johannesen loudly proclaimed, "This is an omen from the gods: Odin."

Not being superstitious, the Colonel could not share Johannesen's jubilation, but he thought it to be quite coincidental that a magazine, one that is not popularly referred to that was purchased on the spur of the moment, would have a detailed article on the geographic area to which they were enroute.

At the wheel Tod was wondering, "What is that loon hooting about now?"

Approaching the lighthouse at Point Reyes, which could be heard but not seen, Tod was given further instructions on the adjusted course from the erratic compass reading. Rounding the Cape of Kings, the Colonel took control of the wheel because the fog was thick and there was a six-foot following sea. About three-fourths past the southern end of Point Reyes, the *Sea Swallow* sailed out of the fog bank and was swathed in brilliant August afternoon sun rays as a clear blue sky shone overhead. The pillowing fog bank poetically caressed the parched, golden hills to the port, and the crew acknowledged this extraordinary scene among themselves. The water was incandescent with breaking white foaming wave crests, and the rowboat was filling up with water, threatening to capsize.

"Maybe we should have left it at Bodega Bay," thought the Colonel.

Johannesen, thinking realistically for a change, wondered out loud, "She might not make it."

It was hypothesized that even if the skiff were to completely fill with water it would not sink, since it was made of wood. Rounding Chimney Rock on the east side, fishermen who have nearly a century of knowledge of the area pass on the west side of Chimney Rock, perilously close to a reef, but save about a mile in traveling time. The rowboat trailing with only a few inches of freeboard, the *Sea Swallow* and its crew were approaching the Saint George's Fishery, where mostly Mediterranean Monterey fishing boats and one-cabin cruiser outrigged with commercial fishing gear were moored. It was so foggy that the fishermen did not venture far that day and returned early to celebrate their annual salmon party. Accompanied by the standard grumblings, Johannesen and Tod pulled down the storm jib and the mizzensail.

Bob Moore was with the merrymakers entertaining the fishermen with his folk songs of fabled lore at the green fishery shed that is supported above the water by wooden pilings when the *Sea Swallow* pulled along side the pier on the east side of the building. The fishermen, catching sight of the schooner, remarked, "It looks like the *Santa Maria*," because of the brown paint that gives the impression that the hull was made out of wood. For a finale, Moore tried to accompany the fishermen through a rendition of "Santa Lucia," but the fishermen had trouble following the guitarist and the guitarist had trouble following the fishermen.

The musician-poet was safely assisted onto the *Sea Swallow* by the fishermen, and the schooner pulled away from the pier and anchored out near an area called Drake's Beach. The fishermen, who are summer residents at Drake's Bay, have their fishing boats secured to a cable or nylon line that is connected to a fifty-five-gallon drum full of concrete or an oversized anchor. This is necessary because the surge in the area is strong and reverberating, and will break loose an ordinary anchor from the sandy bottom in due time. The mooring line—cable or nylon—is held to the surface of the water by a buoy made of that ever-useful substance, Styrofoam, or by large plastic jugs, so when the fishing boat returns the buoy is caught by a boat hook or by somebody simply hanging over the side of the boat, not that differently from how buoys are caught by deckhands for derrick, lay and jet barges in the Gulf of Mexico or at any offshore petroleum field like the North Sea or the Bering Sea off Alaska.

The water-laden rowboat was hauled alongside the schooner and was bailed out once more.

Not satisfied with the culinary abilities of anyone aboard, Johannesen took over the detail as the Colonel and Tod began to attend to the fishing gear that would be employed in the morning. Moore was strumming his guitar, and the dog was snugly curled in the galley near his master. Cigarette smoke from the Norwegian and the musician-poet began to fill the cabin of the *Sea Swallow*, and the entire crew felt a natural elation by just being at the isolated element-bound and historically linked area. During and after dinner, Johannesen took the role from chronic critic to creditor. "How was the meal? Did you like it? Not bad," he would say while the crew was eating. Nobody had bothered themselves to fill his vacant role.

As the evening continued, Johannesen took out his harmonica and began to produce German, Norwegian and English sea chanteys. He also knew a few American folk songs; then Moore would join in with his guitar, another crew member would also vocally join in, and the crew of the *Sea Swallow* inadvertently made a memorable evening.

"Johannesen," addressed Moore. "Was Fusco supposed to meet us today?"

"No. Why do you ask?"

"I thought I saw him."

Tod was leafing through the adventure magazine, looking at the photographs, and thinking to himself, "This place sure looks familiar."

"Oh, really? Where?" continued Johannesen.

"On the way down here, in the fog."

"Could've been him."

"He was wearing a tall hat like you see the pilgrims wear around Thanksgiving, and he had a lantern on the end of a stick."

"Someone at the Boat Center probably told him we were here."

The Colonel had the brass foghorn on his lap and held a rag soaked with ample amounts of Brasso from an open can that he was careful not to tip over. As he listened to the conversation he polished the bugle-like instrument.

After the music session Johannesen put his harmonica in his sleeping bag, located a pencil and a pad of paper and began to draw a picture. The other crew members thought the subject matter the Norwegian was drawing was a maritime scene or something related to treasure hunting.

It was neither.

Johannesen was drawing a dogfight between a Messerschmidt 109 and a British Spitfire. When Tod leaned over to see what he was drawing, Johannesen gave him a "What are you looking at?" stare. But when he finished the drawing he readily showed Tod his spontaneous work of pencil on paper.

Not long thereafter the crew of the *Sea Swallow* retired for the evening. Each crew member had his Army surplus sleeping bag. Moore and Johannesen had their night's supply of cigarettes by their sides. This area of northern California can sustain temperatures in the middle forties during the summer months, especially at night. Johannesen began to reinstate his grumblings: "Just like the Second World War, when they made us sleep in the snow."

"Which army was that?"

"Forget it," was the answer.

The ever-vigilant Colonel slept in the wheel house, whereas the remainder of the crew lay to rest in the galley. As the fog began to settle over Drake's Bay, the schooner's metal hull began to pick up engine and screw noises of another boat.

"Hear that?"

"It's a boat."

"Who could that be?"

"What's he doing out in this fog?"

"I'm going to check," said the Colonel.

Stepping outside into the Pacific fog, the Colonel could hear but not see the fishing boat drop its anchor. But what caught his eyes' attention was a light on the beach that seemed to enter one of the caves facing the east. For twenty minutes the Colonel tracked this light. Little did he know that the two attendants at the Coast Guard Station were also tracking the same light.

"Must be one of those fishermen," commented one of the Coast Guard attendants. "They know this area better than anyone else around here." He faintly remembered the other watch mentioning: "If you see an old man wandering around with a lantern at night, leave him alone. Don't follow him."

"You can say that again. Ever see how they run at full steam between Chimney Rock and that reef? It's probably the old man the other watch was talking about."

"Hey, a few months back, wasn't there a report..."

What neither the Colonel nor the Coast Guard attendants were aware of was that Lester had just arrived at Drake's Bay. The tidal basin resident, fatigued from the long ordeal, chose not to put out his crab trap. After a meal of sardines, crackers, cheese and tomato juice, he too retired for the night.

Johannesen's constant haranguing about the rowboat had begun to affect the Colonel's subconscience, unbeknownst to him.

In his sleep the Colonel was on the *Sea Swallow*'s aft deck with the First Mate, who was voicing his usual opinion about the rowboat that was on a tow line. As Johannesen was talking, the rowboat began to move closer and closer, ("We ought to cut it loose, Colonel"), faster and faster toward the stern of the schooner.

When the pointed bow of the speeding skiff was ready to strike the schooner's stern, Johannesen yelled, "It's going to sink us! It's going to sink us!" The Colonel was awakened by the sound of the rowboat's bow knocking on the schooner's hull.

Petrified that the nightmare could transform itself into reality, the Colonel made it to the *Sea Swallow*'s aft deck, half expecting to find a vengeful skiff attacking his sailboat, but instead found the skiff quietly alongside the schooner.

Although the crew of the *Sea Swallow* had desired to be awakened at five in the morning, the Colonel, seeing that the fog had not yet lifted at that hour, decided to let them sleep. Everyone was awakened when the Italian-American commercial fishermen began arriving at Saint George's Fishery and the fishermen began to loudly converse with each other.

"I cannot lie. I saw something last night."

"You always see something."

The fishermen were boarding a skiff to transport themselves to their fishing boats that were tightly hanging off the mooring lines because of the wind, waves and current.

"I'm the only one who'll talk about it."

"*Tu sempre diventare cosi eccitabile.*"

"*Sono uno desperato? Uh!*"

"You act like one."

"I'm going to the Coast Guard about this."

"What can they do?"

"Whose boat is that?" He referred to Lester's custom-made pitch-colored sloop.

"*Non saccio.*"

The attendants at the Coast Guard Station were also examining Lester's sloop.

"Come here. Take a look at this."

"They come in all shapes and sizes."

As the engine was warming up, the crew of the *Sea Swallow* was finishing the standard breakfast of bread, peanut butter, jam, coffee, milk and cigarettes. Soon thereafter the anchor was weighed to the melody of Johannesen's bellyaching. The *Sea Swallow* underway sailed past Lester's sloop, and had the crew babbling in bafflement.

"Ain't that Lester's sloop?"

"What's he doing here?"

"I told ya he'd be up here. I told ya!"

"He came all this way—what kind of auxiliary has he?"

Departing the protected confines of Drake's Bay, the *Sea Swallow* in three- to four-foot seas cast out its two trolling cables with about ten stubber lure attachments on each cable. Then the *Sea Swallow* began the laborious process of moving slowly to and fro where the crew speculated the elusive salmon might be. Changing directions had to be done slowly and carefully so as not to foul the twin trolling cables. Tod held the wheel watch almost exclusively while the other crew members attended and kept an eye on the trolling cables.

Bob Moore began to string his guitar and Johannesen thought by touching the cables that a fish was on the line. The Colonel and Johannesen began to reel in the cable by hand on the girdie and the Norwegian's guess proved to be true. A sleek, glittering silver coho salmon without any exterior spikes, unlike the more primitive sea bass better known as "bottom fish," was struggling to free itself from the hook. Johannesen was on his stomach trying to place the large catch net under the fish so that if it did succeed freeing itself from the hook it would not become "the one that got away." Anyway, it was desired for the fish to fall into the net because if the salmon was allowed to flop and writhe around the deck the slippery fish would be difficult to handle and could find its way back into the water. As it turned out, the fish freed itself from the hook and fell into the net.

The cable once more strung out, Moore was still tuning his guitar and now Johannesen thought that the other cable had a fish on it. Reeling in the cable again, Johannesen's projection proved to be true. Tod was so occupied holding the boat on course that he was unaware that the boat had a fish on the line until it was aboard in the net.

"Hold'm there, Colonel. He's getting away."

"I'll try to bring him up a little more."

"What's all of this noise about?" thought Tod.

"Tod, let the wheel go for a minute," said the Colonel. "Hold Johannesen's feet so he don't fall in."

"What's he doing now?" Tod experienced a moment's hesitation, but seeing the Norwegian giving an earnest effort lying on his stomach trying to net the fish, he readily held his feet. It was surprising how cooperative Johannesen could be when he measured up to the situation.

It was then that the crew realized that at both times when the salmon were caught, Bob Moore had been strumming his guitar and Tod had been humming at the wheel. The musician-poet, examining the fish, was ordered, "Bob, you're bringing in the fish.

Get back to the guitar." Moore made a conscientious effort to allure the fish, strumming his guitar extra hard and singing as loud as he could, to the point where a guitar string snapped. But fate had played itself out; no more salmon were to be caught that day, although a couple of sea bass that stay near the bottom of the ocean were picked up.

As anyone who has dealt with fish knows, once caught they have to be cleaned as soon as possible. This was not being done, and Tod, who was at the wheel, began to complain about this. The Colonel came out of the cabin and took over the wheel so Tod could clean the fish. One fish was of questionable legal size, and Johannesen began to vent his feelings on the matter.

"I don't know about that fish. It looks undersize to me. I say we throw him back before we get caught. What do you say?"

"Throw him back, he says!" Then Tod said out loud, "Throw 'em back! Throw 'em back! That's all you can say. No wonder you never went anywhere in life."

"Explain that to the Fish and Game people when they catch us—I've at least warned you. Anyway, they've been out on the deck too long."

"Which ones do you want to throw away?" asked Moore.

"All of 'em."

"Hey, Colonel, what do you think of that?"

"What's he chattering about now?"

As he has found himself many times in the past without a friend, Johannesen called for his faithful companion. "Dog! Dog!" The mongrel was soon as his master's side.

The Colonel was giving instructions on how to clean fish: "Make sure you get the gills and the vein by the back bone."

The Colonel also instructed Tod to leave the head, fins and scales in place and when the fish was placed in the ice in the large Styrofoam box in the forward hold, to make sure the fish was set straight. If the fish became crooked in the ice, it would lose fifty percent of its value, or, worse yet, not be accepted at all. This Tod did, all the while Johannesen—from a distance—disapprovingly looked on.

Entering Drake's Bay late that afternoon, the crew of the *Sea Swallow*, along with the other commercial fishing boats, had an opportunity to have another extra-close look at Lester's sloop and what he was doing. He moved his boat and tied it alongside the Coast Guard pier about 1,000 feet south of the Saint George's Fishery pier, harvesting the green kelp seaweed for that evening's meal, boiling it in sea water and eating it, similarly as spinach is eaten. He gave every passerby a friendly wave and a smile, then continued his work.

The *Sea Swallow* anchored, it was agreed to save the salmon and to eat the undersized fish and a sea bass and to use what was left of the skate as bait in the crab traps. Within an hour fifteen good-sized crabs, dungeness, red-and-yellow spotted crabs, were hauled aboard snapping their claws and hissing until they were boiling in the pot while the entertainment and news radio 7.5, KCBS San Francisco, was airing a Giants baseball game. Lester also had his transistor radio on KCBS and was listening to the same baseball game, and he, too, had three good-sized crabs boiling in the pot. The Coast Guard attendants, also listening to the Giants losing on the radio, remarked, "This team hasn't won a home game since we've been here."

"Glad I'm not a Giants fan."

The Coast Guard attendants were also observing the visitors and regular fishing boats in the bay.

"Did you see that old man pull in the seaweed today?"

"I understand it can be eaten like collard greens."

"We ought to try it. Must be pretty cramped in that boat of his."

"I saw his mast from here, walked over to take a look at his boat. He's a real old-timer. Wears a blue beret."

"What did he have to say?"

"Not much. Only that he was leaving. Boat's small. Says it takes him wherever he wants to go. He was gathering seaweed."

Everything was peaceful aboard the *Sea Swallow*. Tod finished cleaning the galley after "chef" Johannesen, and instead of throwing the leftover fish bones, crab shells and fish heads overboard, he placed them on the forward hatch by the bow. The fish and crab remains were to be utilized as additional crab bait. Back in the cabin, Tod resumed his reading of the adventure magazine, and his thoughts were based upon the area's rarefied location.

Here we are...north of San Francisco, in the middle of nowhere....Part of his crew were some Devon boys in their teens, a few who were in their twenties....

The Colonel and Bob Moore with his guitar on his lap were discussing past treasure-hunting expeditions in Mexico.

"That old codger was going to leave you in that crater when he found out his wife and that goon double-crossed him."

"I was afraid he was going to throw me in there with you."

The Spanish bark Don Francisco de Zarate *was captured.*

"That's why I wanted you to keep an eye on him. I thought I was never going to get out of there alive."

"I knew it was a mistake to trust him."

The Cacafuego, heavily laden with Peruvian silver, was captured, continued the adventure magazine.

"Since he showed us the place, we can go there ourselves the next time. We'll sail to..."

Exactly then Tod put two and two together. "These pictures, the white cliffs, that's here—Drake's Bay!" Tod was going to bring this to the attention of the other crew members and said the word, "Hey," but they were involved in making vocal plans about the next treasure-hunting adventure to Mexico.

"We're going to have to hire a guide. Remember how those Apaches were ready to scalp us?"

"I speak enough Spanish," said Johannesen. "We should be able to get by with a phrase book."

Lester, his sloop now alongside the Saint George's Fishery pier, climbed the ladder and hoisted an alcohol lamp on a stick from the sloop with a string, then from another string pulled the metal detector onto the deck. The lantern lit, Lester began his search, for it was his theory that searching for something hidden for four hundred years at night had a quaint degree of extra chance because during the day there is too much to see with too much light. With only limited vision and the fact that it was night his latent sensory instincts, which are most important in this specialized method of search, would be fully utilized, augmented by the battery-powered metal detector.

Wanting to catch a breath of fresh air and re-examine Drake's Bay to compare it with the photographs in the magazine, Tod stepped outside onto the aft deck. The boat's wooden steering wheel on the starboard side, the boat's mizzen mast boom overhead, he was greeted by the sharp presence of dew that had settled heavily on the boat, and by a crystal clear night. The Milky Way galaxy had arched over the blackened firmament like a twinkling aureole that cascaded into the cliffs and sea. Indeed, this was the place mentioned in the magazine: the white cliffs, the geographic points, were the same as in the adventure magazine's photographs. Tod walked toward the forward hatch near the bow, and there he was stunned into a quasar reality. The fish heads, bones and crab remains glowed a phosphorescent reddish blue; the fish eyes were as if they were following Tod's movements, the fish mouths were open as if ready to strike. Even the teeth glowed. The claws of the crabs were also poised as if ready to strike, and for a moment Tod was struck by a soulful, primeval fear, then he incredulously stared at the lifeless fish and crabs to verify what he was looking at. The spell was broken by voices on the aft deck.

"The light! Look! It's over there."

"That must be the fellow I saw coming down here."

"Could that be the same light I saw the other night?" thought the Colonel out loud.

"Let's take the boat, Colonel. I'll row," offered Johannesen.

The three men piled into the rowboat with the dog in close pursuit, making way toward the elusive light on shore.

"We'll be back in a little while," explained the Colonel to Tod.

"This is a first," reported the Coast Guard attendant out loud. "I see two lights."

"For cryin' out loud. You sound like Henry Wadsworth Longfellow. Must be a reflection off the windows. Happens all the time in the wheel house on the cutters at night. Haven't you seen this before?" He tried to cancel out what had betided him a week earlier.

"Never took notice of that."

"Johannesen, a little to port. The light is in-between the Coast Guard Station and the fish dock."

Johannesen's back was facing the bow as he was rowing, so he could only see the light farthest away over his right shoulder on the port quarter of the skiff. "What do you mean?" he said. "The light is over there, past the Coast Guard station."

"I was going to say something," confessed Moore, who was sitting on the stern of the skiff facing the bow and could see everything, "but I was afraid you were going to think I was crazy."

"We wouldn't think that about you, Bob," was a comment.

The rowboat with the four occupants from the *Sea Swallow* made it to the location of the first light and, seeing Lester's boat tied up at the fish pier, deduced that it was Lester himself with the lantern. Their reckoning proved to be correct as they put a flashlight on him and Lester responded with an acknowledging hand gesture and the dog in the rowboat let out a few vocal volleys.

All was not well in the Coast Guard station. "They're getting reinforcements. There's a whole boatload of 'em, and a dog too."

"If this continues, we're going to have to file a report and notify someone." He moved his head in disbelief.

The *Sea Swallow*'s rowboat then began to make its way toward the second light, a good quarter of a mile away.

"Where're they headed to now?" thought Lester. The rowboat's direction tipped off Lester about the second light, and he began to walk in that direction. But past the Coast Guard station, as the young sailor had discovered, the passage soon became overwhelmingly precipitous, so Lester had to double back past the Coast Guard station, take a path that led above the cliffs, and monitor the rowboat and the second light's movements from this bird's-eye view.

On the *Sea Swallow*, Tod was also monitoring the rowboat moving toward the second light, but the second light proved to be much more elusive than the first light.

"Where's the first light, anyway?" thought Tod on the schooner.

Johannesen, who was facing the stern of the skiff, could see another lantern light atop of the cliffs. At first he thought it was an illuminating star or planet like the celestial bodies that shone in between the mountains back in Norway, but he then realized that perhaps yet another light had arrived on the scene.

"How far do we have to go?" asked the Norwegian.

"It's getting away."

"There's another light behind us."

"Who can that be?"

"That's got to be the old man."

All heads turned toward the stern to see the moving light atop the cliffs.

"I say our best bet is to follow this guy," recommended the Colonel, referring to the second light.

Johannesen was tiring, so the Colonel took to the oars himself, with the Norwegian and his dog, who was pointing his nose as if to show where to go, on the bow dictating directions and Bob Moore sitting on the stern seat. The carrier of the second light stopped and Johannesen took note. "We're gaining on him. We're gaining on him. He ain't got nowhere to go."

The First Mate of the *Sea Swallow* took a seat beside the Colonel, assisting with an oar as Bob Moore directed the rowboat that was producing a considerable wake. Moore was looking at the oars dip into the water and the gullying reaction the oars caused in the water and said to himself, "Holy smoke! We've really moving out."

The Colonel and Johannesen stopped rowing to check their progress, and the skiff continued to glide forward as the dog was cowering its head under the bow seat.

"This is about as close as we are going to get," said the Colonel.

If the rowboat advanced any farther it would have been in serious danger of being caught in the surf and ending up on the rocks.

The obscure image carrying the candle-lit lantern was peering at his pursuers as if daring them to continue into the rocks. The four occupants of the rowboat could see the outline of the man's aquiline features, his dark garments and the steep cliffs his lantern revealed in the backdrop. The three fellows in the rowboat were too awed at first to put the flashlight on him, and the dog, whimpering, covered his eyes with his paws. When Moore finally thought about putting the light on the image, a gust of wind suddenly entered the scene, the water became choppy, and the Colonel and the Norwegian had to put the oars in a reverse movement to steady the skiff. The man with the lantern whirled around in a half circle with his cloak full blown with air. He moved into the darkness of the cave. The four occupants in the skiff watched on until the last of the lantern light could not be seen any longer.

"Who in his right mind would want to live in that place?" two out of the four occupants of the skiff were questioning themselves in one form or another.

It took more than two hours for the rowboat to make the return trek to the *Sea Swallow.* While the rowboat was half an hour away from the schooner, Lester's sloop was seen sailing across the skiff's bow. But no one was seen at the helm. The Colonel, Johannesen and Bob Moore were too tired to make anything out of this, and they only looked forward to joining the crew member who was sleeping—yet in his mind's eye he had been following everything his comrades had experienced.

By 9:30 ante meridian the Colonel had the coffee brewing, knowing that its aroma would arouse the rest of the crew. A few minutes later cigarette smoke was filling the *Sea Swallow's* cabin and the crew was preparing for another day of commercial fishing. This morning Johannesen was particularly moody as he assisted with heaving the anchor.

"Damn cursed thing! We ought to cut the line. That'd serve ya right," he said, talking to the anchor. His decision finalized. "Get the knife!"

"Joe, that ain't gonna do. Let's get the line tied off."

The anchor line made fast on a cleat, the Colonel maneuvered the schooner with its engine, and the anchor quickly broke bottom and another commercial fishing expedition was underway. Lester's sloop anchored amid the other fishing boats produced the usual murmurs, which lead to the previous night's inconcise excursion.

"You think he had anything to do with that light last night?"

"We put the light on him, didn't we?"

"But that other fellow. With the light over there." He pointed to the location off the schooner's starboard forward quarter as it was exiting the bay.

"Must've been a fisherman or someone from around here." Moore was thinking, "Tod wasn't there. How does he know about this?"

The routine was established: Tod was at the wheel, the Colonel and Johannesen were watching the trolling cables, and Bob Moore was busy tuning and strumming his guitar.

"Dampness. Before you know it my bass strings are going to rust."

Wanting to search for new fishing grounds, Tod suggested, "Colonel, why don't we go over there," he pointed with his right hand to the area at the tip of Point Reyes. The Colonel agreed, and Tod turned the bow of the *Sea Swallow* toward the open sea. Bob Moore took this inopportune time to eat lunch. At the moment the schooner was about to climb a swell, Moore was preparing a glass of milk. He was raising it to his mouth when—splash— a half a glass of milk was dripping down his face and onto his clothes.

"Colonel, how long are you going to let that kid run this boat?" moaned Moore. "He's going to tip us over before it's over."

"Now, Bob," answered the Colonel. "It won't be long before we'll be trolling at the Point."

Arriving at the area off Point Reyes, the *Sea Swallow* wallowed, pitched and rolled no matter which direction the schooner was running. The *Sea Swallow* was not catching any fish, and two members of the crew were becoming very difficult. It was then agreed to anchor the *Sea Swallow* in a cove on the southern end of the cape and try to catch bottom fish that fetched only fifty cents a pound compared to two dollars a pound for the prized salmon, but bottom fish is better than no fish at all and wasting diesel, wear and tear on the boat, and listening to the adjective-sprinkled opinion of the rocking situation by two crew members.

Within half an hour after the anchor was cast off in the protective cove, all of the drop lines, just pieces of nylon string with lead weights or pieces of metal tied to the end of the string, leaders with hooks and bait at the ends of the leaders attached along the strings, were tied to the boat's railing and were cast over the side. Two sportsman's fishing angles were also put into use, and at once the crew members of the *Sea Swallow* began to haul fish aboard: blue snapper and red snapper, a popular type of spiny dorsal fin sea bass. Once Tod just reeled in his fishing rod's line and a blue snapper was on the hook and gave no fight until it was out of the water and in the net.

"Can you believe this? A fish fell asleep on my line!"

An hour after the first fish were brought aboard, the fish stopped taking to the hooks. For some unexplainable reason, Johannesen caught the next three things—affirmative, things, because it was difficult to determine even by someone who had spent decades by the sea if they were animal, vegetable, or both. The first unidentifiable creature the Norwegian brought up caught Bob Moore's eye and he asked, "Hey, Johannesen, what's that?"

"It's a gizz," was the reply.

On the next try, Johannesen pulled up something that resembled a colored jelly fish or shell-less mussel.

"Johannesen, what ya got now?"

"A blob."

On the third try Johannesen brought up something that topped the whole—what is it—bizarre marine catch. It was a round human-skin-colored baseball-shaped organism with many moving spiny legs.

"It's a forget-me-not. Once you've seen it you can't forget it." He reeled in his angle line and said, "I quit. The gods are against me today."

A few minutes later Johannesen was on the main deck of the schooner in company with his dog, looking at Tod with his angle in the water. Becoming somewhat bored with the concurrent situation, the Norwegian decided to initiate some extra curricular commotion.

"Make sure he doesn't get away," warned Johannesen to his fair-sized mongrel. "Watch him. Watch him close," continued the Norwegian as he laid his arm around the dog, patting his rib cage as the hair on the dog's back rose while he growled in anger. "He's moving, watch him. Don't let him get away," and the dog, obedient to his brainless master, was more than ready to rip into Tod from head to toe.

"Johannesen, I'm not kidding one bit. You keep it up and I'll throw you and that mutt in the water."

"You wouldn't throw an old man," he made reference to himself and the ragged condition of his clothes with his equally soiled and callused hands, "in the water," as if saying, "me, a poor little old man," a modified version of the phrase, "me, a poor little boy," that Johannesen had employed some forty years earlier. "Anyway," he continued, "there's sharks out there."

"Should've thought of that before you got that mutt all revved up."

"Keep your eye on him, dog," warned the Norwegian as the dog recommenced his guttural sounds. "Don't let him get away. Watch him. Good dog. Good dog."

"Keep on making a nuisance out of yourself. Just keep it up," and Tod pointed to the water. He reeled in his fishing line and moved to another part of the boat. The dog desperately wanted to "get" the retreating fellow, but Johannesen held him back. "He ain't getting away," said the dog's master. "We'll get him. Don't worry."

Tod began to mumble on his own within earshot of Bob Moore. "That good-for-nothing bum. Vagabond."

"Johannesen's acting up again, is he?"

"That over-aged hippie," said Tod out loud so that everybody could hear. "Leftover beatnik, he is," and his voice echoed off the cliffs of Point Reyes.

"Watch 'em, dog. Watch 'em. Be on your guard," responded Johannesen, whose low-keyed voice could also be heard since sound travels easily on the water, especially in a protected cove.

"Going to check the old man out tonight—or whatever it was?"

"Don't know. It's up to them."

"Got a good look at one of 'em. Zapped him with that flashlight."

"You saw that. Couldn't catch the other one. It's probably Fusco. You know I saw him in the fog coming down here. We couldn't catch him. Then again, it could have been someone from around here. You know Fusco?"

Tod acknowledged this with a pathetic nod of the head and facial expression.

"He was all dressed up. Old-time hat and cloak."

"I know that Johannesen once lived in a cave too," commented Tod.

Moore and Tod were both exchanging pathetic acknowledgments.

The crew, being tired from the long hours on the boat and from the previous night's row around the western end of Drake's Bay, were finding it difficult to keep their eyes open. Although a stiff northern wind was blowing and the ocean was choppy, the cove where the *Sea Swallow* had been anchored was as still as a millpond. The afternoon sunshine had warmed the schooner's deck to the middle seventies, which enticed the crew of the schooner into a restful sleep.

When the crew awoke two and a half hours later, the wind had changed a little to the northwest, which changed the direction of the bow slightly more seaward; but what really mentally rattled the schooner's crew was the sight of Lester's sloop anchored nearby off the stern of the *Sea Swallow*.

"Who's following who, anyway? What's he up to?"

"Gotta wait and see. But if he ain't careful, that floating piece of tar and driftwood is going to be framed in one of those caves."

Being sequestered for three days on the schooner, the Colonel suggested and the crew agreed without hesitation to take a run into Inverness to raise a glass or two. On the drive to town, all eyes were in search of the lantern and its bearers or anything out of the ordinary. No matter how much they tried to imagine, nothing was seen that could fulfill their wishful imagination.

Because of the extra closeness in the station wagon, the topic of discussion changed to personal hygiene as they were nearing Inverness. After a few nasal detecting noises Johannesen was asked, "When was the last time you took a shower?"

The Norwegian had the appropriate retort. "I was going to ask you the same thing. You don't smell like the first rose of summer, either."

Tod, being the youngest member of the group, was receiving some awkward but well-intended assistance in making social contact with a pretty barmaid when ordering the first round of beer.

"We're off the commercial fish boat, the *Sea Swallow*. Have you heard of it?"

Of course the girl had never heard of the *Sea Swallow*, and she moved her head in the negative.

"He's with us too," he said, referring to Tod. The barmaid acknowledged this with a half smile, half smirk; Tod responded likewise. The girl walked into the back room to get the order of beer, delivered it, became paid, politely accepted a tip, exchanged another quick glance with Tod, and that was that.

With crafty movements, Johannesen was shiftily eyeing this dramatic romantic interaction and could not refrain from expressing his opinion upon the matter, putting on quite an exhibition in the process.

"Let someone who has been around show you the finer points in—what's it called—courting, wooing?"

At this particular time of the trip nothing could surprise Tod, and the other crew members were looking at him to see if he would cringe toward the exit. In fact, Tod was interested to see just what this jokester was about to do.

Johannesen walked toward the juke box and then realized that he did not have any coins in his pockets. But the music box's "Make Another Selection" light was on, and he made notice of this with an "Oh" and picked out the title of a very sentimental song, pressed three buttons, and before the music started he publicly dedicated the song to the most beautiful girl in the establishment. The barmaid was blushing various shades of red as the Norwegian sang along with the juke box with his nicotine-tarnished voice.

Other patrons in the tavern were a little embarrassed themselves, but the crew of the *Sea Swallow* had become accustomed to Johannesen's antics.

After the song concluded, Johannesen was again studying the list of songs on the front of the juke box with his lined face for suitable dance music. Not locating one to his liking, Johannesen ordered Bob Moore, "Moore, how about some dance music?"

The electrician-musician took his guitar out of its black leather case, only taking a few seconds to tune the stringed musical instrument, thinking, "This is good enough for him," and began to produce an Irish jig while the Norwegian skipped along with the music. Johannesen's dog was among the audience sleeping through the entire one-man vaudeville act.

After frequenting every bar that was still open in Inverness, the proverbial fishermen piled into Bob Moore's station wagon with the Colonel at the wheel and headed back to Drake's Bay.

"Wouldn't it be nice," suggested Tod, "if Tom was here so that he could give us a rendition of his poetry."

The negative response sent the station wagon weaving from one lane to the other.

"Don't you start that!"

"Don't you get him going. That's the last thing I want to hear is his poetry."

"He ain't even here!"

"I rather like Tom's poetry," explained the Colonel, driving the station wagon along the winding road. "Oh, once in a great while he'll get carried away, but that is to be expected. His repertoire. The emotion he displays. The dynamics of voice. The tears."

Getting out of the station wagon by the Saint George's Fishery, the crew of the *Sea Swallow* came upon Lester walking by with his alcohol lantern burning. He was going to his sloop, which was at the end of the fish pier.

Johannesen was recalling as he saw the old man walking with the lantern, "just like Fasching," when children in Teutonic countries walk the streets the night before Ash Wednesday with varied colored and designed candle-lit lanterns on sticks to ward off evil spirits.

Bob Moore began to ask, "Was that you up there the other night? We were…"

"T'was I," was Lester's simple answer.

For the first time all four crew members of the *Sea Swallow* were able to see Lester's electronic metal detector.

"May be he ain't so nutty after all."

"He stands a good chance of finding something with that."

On the row back to the anchored-out schooner, the four fishermen had no unusual observations or thoughts except for the fact that a summer northern wind storm was approaching.

"*Troppo vento! Troppo vento*," was the exclamation that awakened the crew members of the *Sea Swallow*.

"*Vede alcuni fantasma recentemente?*"

"Haven't seen nothing. Haven't seen nothing. *Troppo vento per pesca!*"

"We'll go out for a while. *Se le ondas troppo alto tornarmo* okay."

"I don't like this. *Qualche cosa non correcto.*"

Three hours after the area's regular fishermen had departed, the crew of the *Sea Swallow* were weighing their anchor. Since the salmon trolling was not proving fruitful and the weather continued to increase in volume, the *Sea Swallow*'s crew modified the plan for the day to bottom fish on the southern end of the cape of Point Reyes. The rowboat was tagging along the stern of the schooner, the reason being the fish catch could be greater if the fishing lines would be cast off in more than one location, and having someone in the rowboat hanging off of the stern of the *Sea Swallow* would produce exactly that.

Just west of Chimney Rock, Lester and his sloop were anchored off a long line. It was obvious that the old man was up to something, and the crew of the *Sea Swallow* was curious to find

out what their neighbor from the tules of the Napa River was doing. To have an intruding view of Lester, the *Sea Swallow* anchored
near the old man's sloop. Johannesen hopped into the rowboat
with two fishing angles, bait and his dog, and Tod paid out enough
line so that the Norwegian was almost on the rocks. With the
rowboat cast off, the remainder of the schooner's crew prepared to
put their drop lines overboard. Before this was completed, a
thump, thump of the wooden bow of the rowboat was heard on
the schooner's stern. Johannesen had pulled himself in with an ur-
gent message.

"I think the old man's found something. He's digging like mad
over there."

Tod offered to accompany Johannesen, and he agreed. "Why
not? Come along."

Boarding the skiff, the dog was voicing his disapproval of the
other person with a slight growl and wary eye while the rowboat
was being rowed backwards toward the Point.

"Make sure that line doesn't get tangled up," instructed
Johannesen, who was rowing from the amidships thwart, to Tod,
who was sitting on the thwart forward of Johannesen. The dog,
not too happy about a number of things, was uneasily sitting on
the transom seat.

The Norwegian was the first to jump into the waist-high water; Tod reluctantly followed as the dog stayed in the little boat
barking in bewilderment. Lester was furiously digging with a
shovel and pick, and his metal detector was lying a few feet away.
To be of any help, two more shovels would be needed.

"I'm going to get another shovel, Joe."

"Bring one for me, too. And hurry up. We can't stay here
long."

On the half walk, half swim back to the rowboat, the dog was
pleading more than arguing with his whines that it was his desire
for his master to also come aboard the small boat and return to the
schooner.

Pulling the skiff to the schooner, Tod requested the two shovels, which were promptly given to him. Rowing backwards, the Colonel paid out even more hang-off line from his end to ensure a short walk in the water as the line went over the bow of the skiff. The other fishermen were returning to Drake's Bay because the wind and the seas were mounting steadily. When they saw Lester's sloop and the *Sea Swallow* with the green rowboat hanging off its stern, practically on the rocks, they suspected that a salvage operation was in progress, or that someone could be in trouble. Someone among the onlookers on their way to Drake's Bay notified the Point Reyes Coast Guard station for possible evacuation.

"What seems to be the nature of the distress?" requested the Coast Guard station a short distance away.

"Some old man in a black sailboat is on the beach. That schooner with the fishing rig, Sea-something, is trying to assist him. I don't know what they're doing. Looks like they're digging from here. It's really whipping up."

"Coast Guard station back: Roger on the weather. Do they require any assistance?"

The Colonel, having his very high frequency radio turned on, overheard this conversation from the stern of his boat and cleared up at least partly the speculative talk.

"Break, break, Coast Guard Station Point Reyes—*Sea Swallow.* Over."

"*Sea Swallow,* this is Coast Guard Station Point Reyes. What seems to be the problem? Over."

"*Sea Swallow* back; we're standing by the black sailboat. The old man's ashore. We're lending him a hand. He needed a couple of extra shovels."

"We understand the weather is picking up. Our anemometer is reading thirty-five knots."

"That's a roger. I imagine within half an hour we will have to pull away from here."

The Coast Guard attendants on watch were not the same

people who had been tracking the lantern lights at night, but they had been informed of what had been transpiring, and overwhelming curiosity encouraged them to make an inquiry that exceeded the bounds of professional interest. "What's going on out there, anyway?"

"*Sea Swallow* back; they're digging out there. Ah—I don't know what for." The Colonel, looking out from the stern of the schooner, could see Lester, Johannesen and Tod frantically digging into the sand, throwing full shovels of sand and pebbles over their shoulders. Moore was holding the schooner's wheel, because even though the *Sea Swallow* was anchored, its danforth anchor was sure to drag on the sandy bottom in the growing seas. "We're with the old man. They're after something. Two of my crew members know him from the North Bay. The Napa River."

"I've got you. You haven't by any chance been tracking a wandering light lately, at night?"

By now every fishing boat was listening on channel 16 with undivided attention. Ships about to enter and leave the Golden Gate and ships traveling up and down the coast were being more than entertained by the conversation.

"Why, yes, we have. The old man's digging on the shore with my two crewmen…*Sea Swallow* to the Coast Guard Station, stand by, please."

"Coast Guard Station Point Reyes standing by with the *Sea Swallow*."

Bob Moore, keeping the boat's position from various landmarks on the Point, informed the Colonel that the *Sea Swallow* was dragging her anchor and that an immediate departure should be executed.

"We've got to get the Sam Hill out of here, Colonel. We're draggin' anchor."

"Coast Guard Station Point Reyes—C.F.A. 5022 *Sea Swallow*. Over."

"*Sea Swallow*—Coast Guard Station Point Reyes. Over."

"*Sea Swallow* to the Coast Guard station: We are dragging our anchor, so we are going to be moving out. I don't know about the old man."

"Affirmative on that. If any additional assistance is required, feel free to contact us. Coast Guard station clear with the *Sea Swallow* standing by on channel 16."

"C.F.A. 5022, the *Sea Swallow* clear with Coast Guard Station Point Reyes."

The fishing boat which had originally alerted the Coast Guard offered to stand by to make sure the three shovelers would not be stranded ashore to face the blowing wind and pounding waves, even though the captain of the assist fishing boat felt that whatever fate befell them in that ridiculous location in their even more ridiculous quest would be to their own entitlement.

The efforts of the three shovelers working frantically before a rising tide that was lapping at their heels and threatening what they uncovered and what they believed to be an unmistakable sign that they had in fact come upon a remnant of what they were searching for: part of Drake's treasure, part of the forty tons of plundered gold and silver that historical annals speculate never reached England, that the adventure magazine claimed the English pirate had buried on the California coast at a geographic area closely resembling the area they were at, a place Francis Drake called "Portus Nouve Albionis" or "Port of New Albion" because the white cliffs and rolling hills that surrounded the bay where the *Golden Hind* had been careened reminded the pirate of Dover.

"We found it! We found it!" bellowed Johannesen above the sounds of the wind and waves.

"What's he yelling about?" asked Moore.

"I think they found something."

"We can't stay here, Colonel."

"I know! I know!"

"How much longer do you want to stay here?" requested Tod to Lester.

"Three more minutes."

He punctuated his answer by raising his left hand showing three fingers. "Three more minutes."

Lester, Johannesen and Tod began to uncover more decayed timbers held together by cast-iron straps and bronze bolts and screws. It was beginning to become inundated by the rising water. Had they in fact come upon ingots, doubloons? The Colonel put the polished brass fog horn to his mouth and blew five distinct blasts, indicating danger. The Doppler effect and the naturally resonant chambers of the Point Reyes cliffs transformed the reedy-sounding fog horn into a resounding instrument of warning. The three shovelers, all of whom were from contrasting backgrounds and had triangular personalities, unanimously interpreted the five sonorous fog horn blasts as:

"The trumpet has sounded! The hour is at hand!"

"That is it," declared Johannesen. "The gods shall tolerate no more!" Bob Moore was trying to keep the schooner in position as the Colonel was paying out the rowboat's hang-off line so the three treasure hunters would not have to battle the incoming water. Lester did not want to chance his luck by swimming to his tarred sloop, so he boarded the skiff, pointing to his boat, and the Colonel correctly understood that Lester wished to return to his sloop by means of the rowboat.

Although Lester was perfectly willing to navigate his sloop on his own and sail away from the jagged rock point, or maybe ride out the storm there at anchor, the fishing boat standing by approached the little sloop and a deckhand offered to cast a small line and tow the sloop away from the point. Lester took the line and the fisherman eased his boat forward, giving Lester ample time to raise his anchor.

By now Johannesen and Tod were aboard the *Sea Swallow,* dripping salt water but indifferent to their wet condition.

"We almost had it. We've got to go back!"

"What did you find out there?" asked Moore.

"A treasure chest, I tell you!" exclaimed Johannesen. "A treasure chest. Ask him," meaning Tod.

At the wheel outside the Colonel was listening to Johannesen's wild claim.

"We found the real thing, Colonel. The real thing. You could see the timbers. We don't need the old man anymore!"

"What's he talking about?" asked Moore to Tod.

"Well, we were trying to get through some wood that was held together by cast irons. Found some other metals—brass or copper—it's been there a while. The water was rushing in when we heard the fog horn, and we had to get out of there. We really ought to go back—after this storm blows over."

Moore's face lit up with expression.

Lester stayed under tow just long enough to be out of immediate danger, then let loose of the tow line and hoisted his main sail. The Colonel called the rest of the crew to witness Lester under sail with what most likely was the custom-made sloop treading along at its best speed.

Bow and stern pitching toward the sky,
This I tell you is not a lie;
Oh, are we going to get it,
Moaned Moore with a sigh.
Like argonauts of old,
So brave, so noble, so bold!

How many men have confronted such seas
That can bring the strongest to their knees.
Where it is difficult to hold a course,
Who are these men that confront nature's force?

Johannesen, I can't help it if your teeth ache, I swear.
To swear will unhappy the gods make.
This man is worse than a fake.

Johannesen, I believe your dog is getting sick.
Don't worry. He'll eat it up to the last lick.

Lester in his sloop, the *Sea Swallow*, and all of the other fishing boats made it to the protected anchorage on the extreme western end of Drake's Bay and safely weathered out the storm there.

At the Saint George's Fishery pier, the Colonel and the other fishermen finally met with the two Coast Guard attendants who were involved with the passing events.

"Hope we haven't put you out of your way," apologized the Colonel.

"We heard about the dig on the Point," he said, gesturing south toward Point Reyes. "Has anyone followed up on it?"

"To tell you the truth, we never went back. They plan," referring to the other crew members of the *Sea Swallow*, "to go back there, but hopefully not with my boat. Draws too much. We were going to head back to the Bay Area, but we're going to stay around here and make another surveillance before leaving."

The Coast Guard attendant then revealed to the Colonel his futile chase of the phantom and how he almost fell into the water and the skipper of the *Sea Swallow* added to the conversation how he noticed a single stray light on a foggy night when they heard a boat running in a dense fog and dropping its anchor. Then the Colonel continued about the night when there were two stray lights in the vicinity of the Coast Guard station and the Saint George's Fishery shed. When the Colonel recounted how they almost cornered the man with the lantern after they had identified Lester, "he comes from the same part of the woods as we do, from the North Bay area near Vallejo," the young sailor began to shake all over. The Colonel closed the conversation with, "It could have been anyone, a fisherman or one of my crew members, friends, Fusco. We have an artist aboard—Johannesen—and he has this friend who goes out of his way to create a stir. We don't have anything definite."

Johannesen, working on the bow of the schooner, overheard this conversation and suggested, "I've heard or read somewhere that there is a Renaissance or historical society that is connected with this place. Who knows? It could be them doing some on-the-scene investigation." The Colonel thought that Johannesen was splicing lines—since he was the only one in the crew who knew how to do so—or repairing fishing gear; something of a nautical nature. But this was not the situation at all. Johannesen had decided to secure the two kerosene lanterns to sticks that were among other things in the forward hold. Lester was doing quite well with a lantern on a stick. Bob Moore saw somebody in the afternoon daylight in a fog bank with a lantern on a stick, and whoever it was disappeared into a cave with a lantern on a stick, and the batteries in the only flashlight had a few minutes of energy before being expended. Anyway, the lanterns had much more illumination radius than a flashlight, and the crew of the *Sea Swallow* had agreed that the search for whatever was not over.

The Coast Guard attendants bid them *adieu*, saying "We'll be on duty in thirty minutes. If anything comes up we'll give you a shout."

"Glad to meet you fellows. We'll be standing by on 16."

Late that afternoon Lester sailed by the anchored schooner and asked a favor that completely took the crew of the *Sea Swallow* by surprise. He wanted to know if it was possible that a line could be put on so as to hang off of the stern of the schooner. The favor was granted, and Lester was asked if he needed anything else, food or water. Lester simply nodded his head a few quick times in the negative direction.

At twenty-one hundred hours, while Tod was stargazing, "the Big Dipper is here; the Little Dipper is there; at the end of one there is Polaris—now where is Polaris?" he experienced a split-second scare when he noticed the sloop approaching the stern of the schooner without its sputtering auxiliary engine running or its sails hoisted. Lester was pulling in his sloop by hand. Tod walked to the stern of the schooner and shaped his mouth to ask, "What are you doing?" But before he could say anything Lester pointed to the hills due north over the schooner's bow where a multitude of lit lanterns were roaming about.

Quickly Tod cast away Lester's hang-off line and summoned the crew from deep within the smoke-filled bowels of the *Sea Swallow.* They were in the depths of a profound discussion about the stratagem of past, present and future venturous expeditions.

"Come see—right away. You won't believe it!"

After a five-second glance it was spontaneously decided upon that an immediate investigation was in order. Without further delay, the Colonel, Johannesen and Tod rumbled into the now-leaky skiff.

Before Tod entered the skiff, Johannesen requested, "Bring those two lanterns I put together. They're on the bow. I tied sticks on the handles." Tod did not know what was being explained until he went forward and came upon the lanterns attached to the sticks. Handing the lanterns to Johannesen, the Colonel asked, "Aren't you coming along, Bob?" as he saw Moore standing on the schooner's aft deck.

"I'm gonna let you guys tackle this one."

At this moment Johannesen's hound began to howl and lament as if his master was about to leave forever, never to return. "But I'll tell you what, though: I ain't putting up with this all night," said Moore as he pointed to the dog by his feet.

The rowboat hastily made it back to the stern of the schooner, where the dog gingerly jumped four feet down to the rowboat. The Colonel and Tod each manned an oar as Johannesen bailed out the skiff with an empty coffee can that caught Moore's attentive eye.

"Looks like a one-way trip to me."

Be that as it may have been, the skiff continued to disappear into the darkness, scooping its way toward Drake's Estero Schooner Bay, causing counter-clockwise curls in the water as the dog, wagging his tail, sat on the transom seat like an ancient Egyptian statue.

"*Sea Swallow*—Coast Guard Station Point Reyes. Over."

"C.F.A. 5022, the *Sea Swallow* to the station calling."

"Coast Guard station back; is this the Colonel?"

"He and the rest of the crew are gone. It's me. The guitar player—Bob Moore."

"Do you see the lights on the hills directly ahead of your bow? They're everywhere."

"I know—I see them. The Colonel and the others are following the old man in that direction. They feel he has an inside track on things."

"What happened to the findings at the point?"

"They figured that was a diversionary tactic Drake had set up to have them or anyone who came close to the treasure done away with."

"Do you have any information on what or who is responsible for those lights over there?"

"I think those fishermen who board at that farmhouse are getting into the act. By the way, how deep is the water in that inlet?"

"It's pretty shallow. There's a sand bar at the entrance."

"They'll find out soon enough…"

Lester, realizing that his sloop could become a new permanent geographic fixture on the sand bar by Schooner Bay, had anchored a few hundred feet from the entrance to the inlet. There he waited until the crew of the *Sea Swallow* rowed by, and he hailed them down. No explanation was needed as to who was doing what or where everybody was going on this remote end of the California coast; it was to the lights o'er yonder in them thar hills that were to be investigated as the now fully loaded rowboat with two bailing cans in full operation plowed forward where most probably 400 years previously English pirates had plied the same waters. Crossing the sand bar, the skiff scraped bottom as the oars churned up sand.

Spotting a favorable beach to land on the western end of

Drake's Estero Schooner Bay, the aged skiff's bow with the dog standing there like a figurehead turned in that direction. Hitting bottom with the bow on dry land, everyone lurched forward as the skiff came to a standstill. Since there were no trees or stumps to secure the skiff to, the anchor line was tied off short on an open wooden support frame and was carried out about twenty-five feet on shore and firmly placed into the earth.

But the dog refused to leave the skiff no matter how much coaxing was applied; he wanted no part in the search for whatever there had been in "them thar hills."

There were three groups of people there that night, a night that few will talk about, a night that few want to remember. The crew of the *Sea Swallow* and Lester caught up with the fishermen, all of whom were carrying kerosene lanterns on sticks. Lester always preferred the pristine-smelling alcohol lamp. But the fishermen had come face to face with another group of men who had a bronze metallic countenance about them, with beards; but it was their attire that had the fishermen more than amazed. They wore sugarloaf hats with a matching satin stripes at the base of the hats' cones, large white collars that overlapped their jackets, large leather belts and loose-fitting trousers. Some of the gentlemen wore crude, buckle-type shoes with torn knee-high white socks, or knee-high boots and cloaks hanging from their shoulders down their backs. The few men who wore the dark clothes had buckle shoes; the other men's attire was not dark but maroon in color, which enhanced their bronze radiance.

The seamen of this group, some of whom appeared to be mere adolescents and others of whom were as brackish beaten as Lester, wore simple plain-colored trousers, shirts, bare feet, and multicolored rags on their heads and leather straps tied off in square knots as belts, similar to the rope Lester wore around his waist. The better-dressed men with the tall hats were carrying candle-lit lanterns on scepters; some of the seamen also had lanterns on sticks. Again Johannesen could not help but recall the days in Europe when children walk the village streets with lanterns during Fasching.

Nobody said anything to each other, for they were caught in a mesmerizing stare of each other's company. Finally the lead officer of the unidentified group asked, "What searchest thou for?"

The fishermen did not breath for the next five seconds, and then they began to inquire among themselves.

"They can talk."

"They look like pilgrims."

"Look like pilgrims, they talk like 'em."

"Don't ask any stupid questions.

"What are we going to say?"

"Could this be a theatrical group?" thought another person.

The group of men looking at the fishermen were thinking, "Their resemblance to the Spaniards is great."

Johannesen, feeling that someone should take the lead out of the garble, stepped forward and asked, "Have you seen—is anyone of you—do you know Fusco?"

Everyone involved with the confrontation except the crew of the *Sea Swallow* had no idea what the Norwegian was talking about.

"Johannesen! Now, how would they know him?" admonished the Colonel.

"Whom doth he speak of?"

"Who's that?"

"*Forse uno uomo Italiano. No!*"

Another person was thinking, "They sure glow like those fish and crabs on the boat."

The Colonel and more than one other person was noticing, "Are these people friends of Lester?" since he resembled them more closely than any of the fishermen. This theory was even more seriously substantiated when Lester and the men from the past were seen exchanging cognizant conspiratorial acknowledgments of head, face and hands.

Precisely then a subordinate officer in maroon apparel completely confirmed the fishermen's suspicions. Taking a cue from his leader, the officer approached Lester and declared:

"When she arrives, let it be known unto Elizabeth to maketh good the proclamation of the brass plate."

Lester bowed his head and simultaneously closed his eyes; he conveyed that he understood. The fishermen with their mouths agape now had the gravest of fears: that an invasion from somewhere, unknown, somehow, unseen could take place.

This line of thought flared until once again the leader of the unidentified group from the past spoke for the last time, deflecting the fishermen from their unwarranted fright.

"Hast thou lost a mascot in these parts?"

Laughing at the unexpected humor and trying to figure out what or whom they had come across, the metallic glowing men were slipping away down the hill into a fog bank, until only a glimmer of their lantern lights could be seen. The fishermen and crew of the *Sea Swallow* with their lanterns gave full chase as fast as they could, but at the bottom of the hill all they could find was gravel in a trickling creek, the bare grass of another ascending hill ahead of them, and no sign of the ephemeral visitors they had just encountered.

A clanking of bells was then detected, and the crew of the *Sea Swallow*, still holding on to their lanterns, made full speed toward the sound. Panting from the run around on the coastal hills, they had come upon a herd of dairy cows.